ABOVE THE CALL

Tabbie Browne

ISBN: 978-1-326-22130-0

PublishNation, London
www.publishnation.co.uk

Other Books by this author

White Noise is Heavenly Blue (Book One of The Jenny Trilogy)
The Spiral (Book Two of The Jenny Trilogy)
Choler (Book Three of The Jenny Trilogy)
The Unforgivable Error
No – Don't!

Visit the author's website at:
www.tabbiebrowneauthor.com

Acknowledgement

The author is very grateful for the kind permission granted to use the Pathfinder Dogs logo and information regarding the dogs.

This Book is Dedicated to

Pathfinder Guide Dog Programme
North Lodge House
Castlehill Road
Wishaw ML2 0RL

Tel: 01698 374973

web address: www.pathfinderdogs.org

Charity Numbers SC0350071/1137722

Founder Anne Royle
Patrons Derek Acorah and Gwen Acorah

PATHFINDER DOGS

WORKING

Spook (Merlin's Brother)
Kambo
Akira

RETIRED

Merlin
Clyde

IN TRAINING / NEW BORN

Willow
Balto
Kayra

IN SPIRIT

Bonnie
Isis

Correct as of March 2015

A MESSAGE FROM THE FOUNDER

I'm now on my second book by Tabbie Browne, as a totally blind person I love that it is available in all formats for people to read. The books are catching, they keep you thinking and make you 'look outside the box'. I enjoy reading Tabbie's books in my limited down time.

As the Founder of Pathfinder Dogs, I'm truly honoured that not only is Tabbie using a picture of Merlin (one of our dogs) but also that she is being kind enough to allow us a few words in her book.

Merlin - has always been an 'old gentleman' even as a puppy. He likes things done his way and is very good at training his humans. Although retired now and enjoying his life of leisure Merlin still appears for public appearances for the charity, and does a wee bit of work with old folk. He allows them to pat him and admire him as if it's his job to be admired.

Being a smaller charity we are always seeking ways of fundraising and raising awareness that the whole guide dog movement was started with German Shepherds.

For further information please refer to the dedication page.

Good luck Tabbie.

Anne Royle & Spook (my four legged glasses)
Founder
Pathfinder Guide Dog Programme

Chapter 1

Tisun was deep in thought away from the rest of the pack. As the team leader he often withdrew at crucial times to formulate the next move. The other spirit dogs were taking a pause from their last assignment but knew the break would be short lived, for there were constant demands on their talents. Although in many areas their tactics were frowned upon, they always achieved a satisfactory outcome and many had been forced to admit that justice would not have been done had they not intervened.

For a moment Tisun paused, then was gone. In seconds he was hovering over the man resting in an armchair and gently positioned himself against his leg. Jack stirred. He wasn't asleep and his mind was going over and over again the recent incident. Radar, his police dog was lying on the floor near him and greeted Tisun on his approach.

"Let's bring him over." was the answer.

The only way all three could communicate was when the handler was asleep for when he was awake he had no recollection of his spiritual connections and put many messages he received down to intuition. Using one of their many talents, it wasn't long before the dogs made Jack's head fall to one side and his spirit floated out.

"Hello again." Jack showed no surprise at the visit for this was quite a normal thing and the three were sharing information on a regular basis on the spiritual level.

They had now all floated away from the house, changing their position constantly for they never knew who or what could be tailing them. When they reached what they considered a fairly safe area they stopped.

Collectively they had all gone over many times what had happened that night and were searching for the next lead.Police dog handler Jack Soames had been sent to a disused warehouse after a passing motorist had rung to say that he had seen a prowler lurking around the place. All had seemed quiet and Jack was thinking it may be a hoax call when a man, well he thought it was a man suddenly

1

appeared in front of him. In a split second he saw that his face was partly covered and some sort of headgear masked his hair. As Jack started to speak, the man pulled a gun and aimed it at Radar but wasn't prepared for what happened next, for the dog pack had received the warning and as the gun was fired, the man felt a terrific force knock him sideways. The bullet missed Radar and caught Jack on the shoulder only causing a flesh wound.

The officer was feeling for his radio as he fell whilst his dog witnessed a scene he had seen many times before but which to the onlooker must have been frightening beyond words. Tisun had not only answered the call, but came in like an express train knocking the gunman to the ground and then holding him there. Although he hadn't seen him, the man had certainly felt him and now was lying face down with the weight of what he assumed was a large animal on top of him, the snarling teeth so close to his head he could hear the warning growl and even feel the hot breath penetrating his head covering. Radar knew his help wasn't required but the question arose as to whether he should appear to have downed the man for the sake of appearances when back up arrived, or leave him writhing on the spot making him look as though he was suffering a mental problem. The gun had flown out of his hand and was a safe distance so the dogs decided that Radar should stay where he was because when the captive tried to explain what had happened, everyone would think he was crazy.

It wasn't long before the place was heaving with people. The ambulance took Jack to hospital whilst another dog handler arrived to transport Radar back to the police kennels.

"I could have found my own way," the dog thought "but if they want to give me a ride I might as well take it." He knew his friend would be in good hands and was in no danger and now he could resort to the humour his friends in the pack shared in difficult times which was what helped them cope in many situations.

"So," Tisun addressed Radar and Jack "the man's known to you?"

They were hovering over a stream hidden in woodland, but prepared to move in an instant.

"Very much so. We call him Bill Bungle."

Keen to hurry on to the important facts Tisun said "Because he cocks everything up I imagine."

Jack laughed. "Everything. Don't think he's pulled a job off properly yet, in fact..."

"Yes OK." Tisun cut in "it's not him is it?"

"It's what was there as well," Radar added.

"Precisely. Now go over it again because I came in from the side but knew something was behind him. I felt it went as soon as I got there."

Radar put his mind back to the moment. "As the man appeared, there was a strong presence behind him, not in any form, not even in spirit but it was there and it wasn't good."

"Did you get any feeling Jack?" Tisun didn't expect that he did but had to check.

"No, but it was all over in a split second and when he pointed the gun at you" he indicated towards his dog, "I was only looking at the physical."

"Well Jack, we had picked up something around the warehouse recently which was why we were on the alert but didn't think it would be this."

"You mean you both knew there was something?" Jack seemed a bit put out.

"Jack we get many vibrations, a few are nothing, some are annoying but not dangerous and some that start off as little more than a whisper can turn out to be the most evil threat."

"I know that."

"Yes but you are very earth bound most of the time. How often do you let your mind free? You may be surprised as to how many times we have tried to communicate with you but your thoughts are full of your work or your family, and you don't give us chance to get through."

Jack turned to Radar who nodded.

"Oh the times I've tried to pass you a message but you seem to put up a barrier."

"So the lesson is to take some time to open my mind." Jack understood but it was difficult sometimes with the pace of life to slow down for a moment.

Tisun draw the communication back to the important fact.

3

"Well, we believe something or someone has been starting to use the warehouse as a base. We've done a couple of sweeps over it and there's no sign of arms or explosives so we can rule out any terrorism for now. In fact there's nothing to suggest any physical activity which leaves only one other possibility."

Sometimes an evil source would use an area to gather its workers who would start to penetrate the local area with their powers which then spread outwards but usually they had a specific target in mind. The spiritual forces who attacked those on their own level wouldn't need to use earth venues. So this site would need to be monitored frequently until they were sure it was safe.

The pack was on the alert as their leader returned, not wondering where or why he had left for that was fairly obvious but anxious to get moving before one of them may be sent for another earth stint. They all bore some resemblance to their physical image but there were essential differences and their talents finely honed to their particular field. Every so often they would be placed in such a position on earth for the purpose of refreshing themselves with updated methods.

Tisun had covered all fields and was an expert in every area but still needed to keep up with progress and change of earthly procedures. His image was of a very impressive black German Shepherd Dog and not one you would fall out with.

'Mildew', as he was known, a black and tan German Shepherd always worked as a cadaver dog and had been used all over the globe.

Blue, the Cocker Spaniel was top notch seeking out drugs and tobacco, highly intelligent with a lovely nature.

Cello and Noodle, both Beagles had spent most of their earth lives sniffing out alcohol and foodstuffs especially at airports worldwide, a job they both loved especially when they were at the same location.

King, the Border Collie's forte was firearms and explosives. He worked mainly with the army and had been in some of the worst war zones imaginable.

Fleece, aptly named as he air scented any cash, not only in his vicinity but any neighbouring area. It was a joke with the earth handlers that this Springer Spaniel knew how much money each of them had in their pockets!

There is a very good reason why this team of highly tuned spirit dogs revisit earth. If a person smells an aroma, the brain remembers it so it is recognised the next time it is smelled. The scents the dogs acquire physically are stored into the spiritual memory, therefore as new techniques are used, and different commodities are marketed, they refresh their memory banks, then when they encounter such a thing in their spiritual form, it is instantly known.

Tisun had just informed the pack of his conversation with Radar and Jack when a message came through. Mildew was despatched instantly with King as back up if needed. A petrol station attendant was facing a man with a knife demanding the money from her till. The shop was almost empty but the other couple of customers froze where they stood. The girl behind the counter was shaking in fright and opened the till but her hand stopped as she was about the pull out the notes.

"Get him away!" The man shrieked. "Get him away or he'll get the knife."

The girl, almost in tears slowly looked to where the man was pointing but there was nothing there that she could see. But the man could definitely see the wolf like face with piercing eyes, saliva dripping from its tongue, and the teeth now nearly in front of his nose. The look of horror on the man's face combined with him drawing back gave the cashier enough time to hit the alarm.

The threat had passed but the dogs wouldn't let him escape justice by simply running away at this point. King positioned himself so that as the man tried to leave, he tripped him and once he was on the floor, Mildew took over.The man was still trying to get to his feet when the police arrived, two officers taking him away whilst another stayed to talk to the girl and check the CCTV footage. As soon as the earthly law arrived the dogs returned to base, their task complete.

"Where's Fleece?" King asked upon their return to base.

"Looking after old ladies." Blue's eyes showed the mirth. The two spaniels never missed an opportunity to have a little dig.

A message had been received that a family knew their mother was losing money but didn't know who was taking it and were going to set up cameras to try and catch the thief. The spiritual informant knew the pack would resolve it much quicker and more effectively so had contacted them immediately.

Fleece familiarised himself with the layout of the care home where Edna now lived. All one storey with two corridors making an L shape and at the junction of these were the offices and a family room where staff could talk to relatives at delicate times but was often used by staff unofficially to take a quiet break. The dining room led off the main entrance along with a small lounge and there was also another small lounge at the end of one corridor. The laundry was situated at the end of the other corridor and there were several toilets and bathrooms.

Having satisfied himself as to the environment, Fleece found Edna's room, two doors away from the small lounge. She was sitting alone, her mind drifting back to happier days but thinking that there were many worse off. Like so many elderly people, she could remember events back to her childhood and could even sing a song she learned seventy years before, but her short term memory left a lot to be desired.

"Time for dinner Edna. Let's be having you."

The voice made her jump as two of the carers bustled into the room with a wheelchair and soon had her seated in it and were wheeling her down the corridor. Fleece had already located her purse and got the smell of her money. She had taken her handbag with her but he knew there was more cash in the room, and it only took him a second to locate her little stash. In one of the drawers she had a pack of shower gel and body lotion she had been given for Christmas and had pushed some ten pound notes into the packing. But that wasn't all. His nose told him there were more notes pushed down the cushion of her chair and that meant she was either being very crafty, or was forgetting where she had put the last lot and stored some more. Scanning the room he knew there was no more so he decided to go on one of his 'wanders'. He never concentrated on one place which was how he had notched up many successful results where others may have failed.

He checked on the position of all of the staff, many of whom were busy with lunch. Some residents had to be fed in their rooms, but mostly they were taken down to the dining room leaving the corridors fairly quiet. Meal times always needed a lot of staff participation but this dog took nothing for granted so when he saw a visitor walking down the corridor he was right behind her. At first all seemed perfectly innocent. Known to the staff she had told them she was taking some new vests to her mother's room, but when she stopped at the room before Edna's, she paused, looked round then quickly moved on and entered the next.

It was obvious to Fleece that this wasn't the first time she had been here for she went straight to the armchair and slid her hand down the side of the cushion where the money was. She flicked through the notes then took one ten pound note and put it in her bag before returning the rest. The whole operation was so quick she was out again in less than a minute not realising she was being followed.

That may have been enough for some observers, but Fleece didn't close the book there, as there was a possibility that she wasn't the only one helping herself to Edna's money. To him this was the lowest form of theft, but for now he had his nose going in one direction to see if she repeated the process before leaving. Not this time. With a '"Bye' called to the busy staff she left the building.

Fleece returned to base for a quick update saying he needed time to do the job without being content with the first result as there could be more going on but was greeted with Mildew saying he was definitely being recalled to earth for his next term. The location was North America and that was of little consequence in some ways but inconvenient in others as the spirit dogs could communicate at any time, but when in body could only be used for tasks when the physical was asleep to leave them free to roam at will. Also if they were pulled back to body abruptly by being woken, they may be in a situation difficult to leave. At such times, Tisun called upon his 'helpers', dogs that either had no wish to be pack members or didn't have sufficient skills to be part of the team but they were useful in instances such as the petrol station. Some only needed to use their image to achieve the results and never worked alone, they were always accompanied a team member.

"Better tell Gerald to stand by."

"Hmmm" the reaction was unanimous.

"He will do as he is told," Tisun reminded them although he knew it wasn't a popular choice.

Gerald was a Rottweiler, not vicious but liked to have his own way. He had been used a few times when a ferocious image was required to hold a prey but had to be ordered to stand down when the result had been achieved. It was a joke with the pack that whenever they mentioned him it was always followed with "Put him down boy!" but that was when they weren't faced with him actually working with them.

"As long as he doesn't get put with me" was Fleece's thought as he returned to the home, thankful that this was an assignment he could manage perfectly well alone. The residents were just finishing their dinner and the staff were taking some to the toilet or be changed before putting them in one of the lounges or going back for an afternoon nap in their own rooms. Edna was one of the last to finish eating and it was usual for her to be taken to the larger lounge where the carers could keep an eye on her. She could walk, and often like to go for a little stroll down the corridor but she was so slow that the staff wheeled her to save time especially when they had the other people to see to. She wasn't given a zimmer frame so when she was put on one of the chairs she couldn't move about on her own. With the aid of her stick which was in her room and the handrails along the corridor she liked to take a few steps to keep her independence but it was only when family came that there was anyone with the time to do it. Permission had been obtained to move her in the chair, and so she was becoming less mobile as the months slipped by.

Fleece was in her room now contemplating. He had chosen not to do anything when the visitor had stolen the money this time as he had a gut feeling there was more to it and patience would have to be employed. His senses were on alert and it wasn't long before a carer entered the room. At first she seemed to be tidying up, but then went to the wardrobe and started sliding the hangers along the rail as if looking for a specific item. Then she rummaged on the floor going through shoes and various oddments. On checking she was alone she quickly took something out of her pocket and stuffed it into one of the shoes which she put back with its partner. After closing the door she left the room quickly.

8

The dog hadn't only been watching her, he had been inside the wardrobe, and although it wasn't his prime sense, knew exactly what had been deposited, obviously for later use. It was a small quantity of drugs. This posed more questions. Were they her own and she didn't want to be caught with them, or had they been planted for someone else to find? One thing was for sure, there was no way he was going to leave this until it was completely sorted and Edna's welfare was assured.

He now sent a message to Blue who joined him for an instant then left to do a complete search of the building. When he returned, the news was partly what Fleece had expected but not on such a large scale. There were drug deposits, also traces of where they had been all over the home. The kitchen seemed clear, traces in the surroundings of both lounges, but mainly in the rooms. An unpleasant picture was starting to form in Blue's mind and he hoped it wasn't true. Fleece needed to know now if other residents had been the victims of money theft and called on spirits from the human side, mostly resident's relatives who had already passed and were staying near their loved ones. The answers proved the dogs were on the right track which disgusted them even more.

A message was sent back to Tisun to ask that Blue stayed on this job until it was brought to a satisfactory conclusion and justice done. The answer was that he could but may be called away to cover other jobs if necessary. The spaniels had no worries over how they would expose this, for they had many skills at their disposal but timing would be the key factor even if the whole pack had to come in for the kill, in which case they would want it to be before Mildew's recall. This was going to be a first in their experience but they would make sure it would never happen again if they had anything to do with it.

Tisun was always kept informed when any member of the pack was out and he summed up the possibilities of the drug situation. Of course there would be prescription drugs in that kind of establishment but Blue had also detected hard drugs, but that didn't rule out the fact that someone with access could also be selling any of the controlled drugs.

While waiting for further information his mind turned back to the warehouse. There certainly was some kind of activity there but nothing that could be monitored for it seemed to occur at very irregular intervals. It was definitely not of a physical source but he knew that many operations started in this way and gradually drew in pawns from the earthly world to do their dirty work, after which the fools would be discarded. Most were promised wealth or power but it was never going to be and they only realised that when it was too late. He had made a few quick visits and noticed several trails an entity leaves but at this stage he knew it would be unwise to follow such a lead for often this was laid as a trap.

Fleece was waiting to find out who would pick up the package from Edna's shoe, half expecting it to be the visitor thief, while Blue was examining every inch of the rest of the home, something he always did after the first cursory inspection. He learned which patient required, or was written up for each particular drug, which member of staff signed for administering, and then concentrated on the exact location of the illegal drugs. The office appeared to be clean but the main scent initially led him to the laundry room and the visitor's room. On examining all the bedrooms he found that certain residents also had remaining signs that the hard drugs had been in their rooms. Also Edna wasn't the only one with a package waiting to be collected.

When Tisun learned that this wasn't just a simple theft situation he immediately requested that some of his back up dogs could be available if needed, not giving them any idea of what was involved.

His senses on full alert, Fleece knew someone was about to enter the room and sent a thought message to Blue who joined him instantly. The door opened slowly and one of the domestics entered the room carrying a mop as if to use it, but quickly went to the wardrobe, took the package, put it in his pocket and left. The dogs followed him to the small room where the cleaning equipment was stored where he left the mop, and transferred the package to an inner pocket. From there he went to the next room to get his jacket. He walked down the corridor and, popping his head round the door of the office said "I'm off then, see you tomorrow." The manager was on the phone and just raised her hand by way of acknowledgment, and he was gone.

The situation now wasn't simply to make sure someone was caught stealing money from the residents. There was definitely a drug problem going on, not only with the staff but possibly involving visitors. At first glance the woman may have just been taking money from Edna, but they had to check that she had no connection with the other two. Ten pounds wouldn't have gone far on its own, but she could be lifting small amounts so as not to be detected. It could be coincidence but it seemed strange for all the visits to the wardrobe to happen within such a short space of time and if several were involved it could be a bigger operation.

Blue suggested it seemed too complicated for a normal purchase. He had witnessed many handovers, some in full view of the public, so why be so covert with this. There were plenty of opportunities for staff to trade but one point did seem plausible. If regular checks were made or staff searched, nobody could risk being caught with the stuff on them so to place it in residents belongings would make sense, but then why wouldn't the buyer leave the money in the allotted place for the dealer to take as they left the packet. This showed another fact. No money was left so the arrangement had to be controlled from outside and they were using the home as a cover, a trading post. Also, at this stage it was probable that it was the residents' money that was funding it.

When a vessel travels through water it leaves a wake, and as a bodily or spiritual form moves through the air it also leaves a trail. This lasts for a while but gradually closes so that it is easier to follow someone soon after they have left.

Tisun sent Mildew to follow the visitor while he trailed the domestic. The carer was still on duty so Blue was keeping a close watch on her, leaving Fleece to guard Edna's room and also be alert for any money movement.

The woman had walked the short distance to a house where, once inside, unloaded a tidy sum of notes. The man counted it then sent a message to the carer which simply said 'Place'. She was about to leave when he got up and grabbed her by the throat.

"What are you playing at?"

The woman could barely speak "I don't know what you mean." she gasped.

His answer was to bring his hand across her face so sharply she fell to the floor. Slowly he picked up the ten pound note she had taken from Edna and waved it in her face.

"It's bloody well marked you stupid cow." he screamed. "Why didn't you notice?"

She was trembling from fright and amazement.

"B-b-but it was clean, I looked."

"Then what the frigging hell is that?" he thrust it in her face and sure enough the name of the home was stamped across the top.

"That wasn't there, I swear." She couldn't explain it because it hadn't been there before, Tisun was projecting the image so they were seeing what he wanted them to see.

"Keep out of there." He shouted as he took out his lighter and held the flame at the corner of the note, then dropped it into the ashtray where it became ashes. "Just do the other ones if you can be trusted not to cock it up."

It wasn't long before Mildew traced the domestic to the same address and the dogs soon worked out the amateur operation. Obviously the 'boss' had a hold over all the others, forcing them to carry out his orders, but whatever that was wasn't important to them now, although it may rear its ugly head in the future.

So the system was that the older woman would go round stealing from the easy source of elderly people. She was known at many homes by different names, sometimes pretending to be a relative of one of the residents suffering dementia, and at others posing as a visitor for those who didn't have any family visits. The carer would steal the prescription drugs, and so that she didn't get caught would deposit them immediately in set places, like Edna's shoe. The lad would lift them just before going off shift and take them to the dealer straight away. This meant that this petty criminal was getting the drugs free which he could then sell. This income along with the nice steady supply of cash from the woman provided the funds for him to buy class A drugs which he then supplied to eager users.

Sending Mildew back to base, Tisun met with the spaniels.

"Think we've squashed that one for now." He said referring to the set up.

"No hard drugs then, but I traced some." Blue felt his efforts had been in vain.

"Well anyone coming in could have the scent on them if they are users and who knows, they could even have had a blast while they were here, but you've found no actual stash have you?"

"No. Not this time."

"Well let's hope the thieving stops for a while, but in the meantime we must just make sure those two staff get moved. Do you want to do it?"

"Rather, it's our job after all." Both spaniels replied in chorus.

"See you back at base, and don't make too much of a meal of it." And he was gone.

"Which do you want?" Fleece asked.

"I'll have the lad if you like." Blue's tail waved as though he was going to enjoy this.

With Mildew's guidance, Blue located the domestic. This dog had a naughty talent which he now used. He sidled up to his prey and started to disturb the air into waves around him. With his tail swishing to and fro at a steady rate it wasn't long before the lad was swaying and feeling very sick, and the more he tried to stabilise himself the more Blue swished, to and fro – to and fro.

With his head now over the toilet, he babbled, "what have you given me? It was bad."

Blue left him with the thought imprinted that anything he had from this man would make him ill, and the thought that carrying any drugs would make him equally ill.

"Don't think he'll be going back to work there, or anywhere for a while" he passed to Fleece who had just finished his treatment of the carer. She seemed to be having some sort of reaction caused by touching pills or medicine as they made her start to itch, not a simple itch but a frenzied all over body irritation similar to those unfortunate to suffer anaphylactic shock.

Having carried out their instructions, the two pals exchanged one of their knowing nods.

"Let's tidy up the loose ends." Fleece suggested.

"Absolutely. Come on."

What use the elder woman was going to be to her 'boss' would be debateable as she seemed to have a fixation about touching bank notes in case they burst into flames.

"Well, that will stop her thieving from the vulnerable for a while." Blue's tail now simply waved with satisfaction.

"What kept you?" Tisun demanded as they returned.

"Just finishing off the job." Fleece tried to sound casual.

Tisun eyed them both for a moment. He never did know quite what these two got up to, but they were experts both in their approach and planning and always got satisfactory results so he often chose to leave things as they were and not ask further. But he still gave them one of his 'looks' which always amused them.

Fearing they may have been up against a case of drugs being fed to certain patients who may have had a tidy nest egg stashed away, they were all glad it turned out to be a rather minor job but if it stopped some of the elderly being targeted and used, then it was a successful outcome, for now. Of course there would always be others, the despicable creatures that prey on the vulnerable, but that's what the pack was for.

Chapter 2

Every so often, friends of the pack were invited to a gathering. These consisted of dogs totally in spirit and those at present also in body. Between them they covered all areas of assistance, guide dogs, hearing dogs for the deaf, the helping dogs who would fetch and carry and also those who could detect illnesses. The breed was unimportant, and although the pack kept to their chosen image most of the time, there were some occasions where they merged into one form depending upon the task in hand.

There were several mongrels among the friends but in the spirit sense they were no different. Some referred to being 'in civvies' and much preferred the casual look to the well groomed 'hair in place' lot. Radar was a regular visitor and liked to work quietly without any fuss, just feeding back information as he had enough excitement in his day job. But that was the source which could provide essential leads.

Tisun brought this meeting to order and asked the dogs to keep every sense on full alert in the area of Jack's attack. He purposely didn't mention the warehouse itself as he didn't want the eager ones diving in and ruining any chance they may have of pinning down whatever was going on. The dogs welcomed this latest assignment as it gave them a feeling of contributing the fight against any bad forces, although most of them wouldn't have wanted to actually be in the pack. There had been some who thought they could handle it, but soon fell at the first hurdle on a minor task. Gerald fell into this category but he had his uses so they used him for anything that suited. When they left, Radar hung back and said "There's been no sign of anything substantial, but the air isn't right."

"When did you go?" Tisun asked.

"Only in spirit, I've been confined to general exercise until Jack's back on duty, so I've had to drift off when he was resting."

"Well if there is anything to detect, you'd have noticed. But be careful." Tisun warned. "You could have been observed without knowing."

"I'd thought of that, so made my visits instant." Radar meant that he didn't hang about but did several high speed trips which were done in the blink of an eye or less.

Everyone was silent for a moment then Mildew asked "No trail remains of any kind?"

Radar was silent and everyone looked towards him. His eyes opened wide.

"Not trails, but wait. I must check something." and he was gone.

They were all on the alert now wondering what he had in mind. Within a couple of seconds he was back almost panting with excitement.

"What is it?" the pack surrounded him.

"I should have noticed before but I was looking for trails."

"Yes?"

"Prints. Impressions in certain places. Haphazard, all over the place, not like a proper set of footprints, although..." he was babbling now just relating his findings but not having the answer, "they were very similar to human footprints but the toes were much longer."

"Well done." Tisun seemed pleased. "You return to Jack now."

Radar knew it was time to go and immediately was at his handler's feet.

"You been dreaming son?" Jack stroked his head. "Your feet have been going as if you were running a marathon."

"If you only knew," Radar thought as he laid his head on Jack's lap and gazed into his eyes.

When the pack were alone Mildew told them his news.

"I'm being sent to Canada." There was a hush so he continued. "But I'm going in tandem."

This brought a whoop of delight among the others. It meant that Mildew would be able to complete his refresher course but not take a full earth body life. He would join another dog and they would work together, but he would be able to leave at any time and return at will. This only happened with the higher skilled dogs such as Tisun, so it was a bit of a promotion for Mildew to be allowed this, also the powers who designated earth lives must appreciate the need for him to be free at all times.

It was a strange situation at first because it meant that two souls were in the same body and there had to be an adjustment period. He had been host to such an arrangement more than once which was a training in itself for the time which had now arrived. He would have to make sure his personality did not affect his partner for he would be there simply to catch up on any latest methods.

This was a tremendous relief to Tisun, especially if the warehouse proved to be an evil concentration area.

There was never a long pause before another request was received by the pack, and quite often jobs overlapped, but this call required every dog as their expert senses were essential. A massacre was occurring at a shopping mall in New York and no one had seen the gunmen. Tisun froze. Something wasn't right. Quickly he ordered Cello and Noodle to do a quick reconnoitre and report back. All hackles were up as they awaited their return and they knew as soon as they arrived that Tisun's suspicions were correct.

"Nothing going on boss." Cello said.

"Just a hoax." Noodle was annoyed but realised the severity of it.

Although playful spirits caused much mischief around them, this had a more sinister feel.

"They were trying to draw all of us well away." Tisun summed up. "That means we're on to something." Although it could have been anything, the leader had the instinct that it had to have some connection with the warehouse, but what?

"I'm going for a quick look." Tisun had gone before any of the others had chance to stop him or ask any questions. He was back immediately.

"Got it."

"Got what?" Normally there would have been some sort of joke about not giving it to the others but they all knew this was not a time for that kind of humour.

"Radar thought he noticed more prints left in the air. I think they are some sort of alarm system."

"What?" was the chorus.

Tisun paused. "Think of security in the earthly way. Rays, sensors that detect movement. Well I think these are spiritual ones,"

"But why?" King wondered.

"A preparation for something they are going to do later?" said Blue.

"But what could it be?" Mildew was deep in thought now.

Tisun was well aware they wouldn't have the answers yet but said "If we knew that…" gave them a moment to ponder then added "it's obvious we have to be diligent, but from afar, although whoever it is must have some idea we are on to them."

Fleece asked "Would it be an idea if none of us went near it and left it to the friends to observe?"

"Good thought, except," Tisun looked round the pack "the others, willing as they are, don't have our honed skills. They may miss something important."

"We could pick the best." Mildew said but changed his mind "no, perhaps not, might jeopardise the whole thing."

"Exactly" Tisun was relieved one of them had worked that much out. "So for now we lie low but we can't relax our interest for a second."

They all gave signs of agreement and were about to settle when another call came in.

After the last episode they were all very wary but they had to check out everything. This was one of the most distasteful to all of them. The report said a man was abusing girls but no more. Tisun decided to take this one himself in the company of the two beagles.

They were soon in the man's living room. The place was untidy and dirty and there were empty beer cans strewn about the floor. They explored the downstairs which was all in a similar state then moved upstairs. The front bedroom contained a double bed which looked as though it was in continual use, the linen not having seen a washing machine for a long time. The back bedroom seemed to belong to a teenage girl due to the contents whilst the box room was full of junk. The bathroom looked as though someone had tried to keep it clean but was losing either the battle or the will. Tisun returned to the girl's room, then to the front bedroom. On the walls were pictures of teenagers, some in very provocative poses but some very innocent looking ones.

"Wonder if one of these is his daughter." Cello was studying them.

"No sign of an adult woman here." Noodle was examining the wardrobe and the drawers.

The front door opening put their senses on high alert. The man came in slowly, went into the front room, threw himself onto the sofa, and pulling a pack of beer out of his bag, opened one and poured it down his throat, followed by a filthy belch.

"And some young person has to live with this." was the thought that ran through the dogs.

"Well, we've sorted this kind of thing before, and we'll do it again." Tisun was tough but still disgusted.

Noodle was thinking of the girl. "If she's still at school she could be home soon."

"Who'd want to come home to this?" Cello asked.

"Possibility she could be at work." Tisun hoped she was not under age if her father took the abuse to a sexual level but that had to be proved yet. Hopefully it was just bullying abuse, in which case the team had their own ways of dealing with it, not always by the book, but that was their business.

Tisun decided to leave Cello in situ and call them in when she arrived during which time he would have hopefully formed a complete picture of what was going on here. He now beckoned Noodle to go with him and they did a sweep of the downstairs back room and the kitchen. All seemed to be in the same state as the rest of the house, apart from the girl's bedroom. Being a terraced house the back yard was fairly small with the usual buildings, originally designed for an outside toilet and coal house. Neither contained anything unusual so the two dogs rejoined Cello who said all was quiet apart from the noises emitting from the lounge.

It was dark before they were aware of the front door being opened very quietly. A girl of about sixteen, dressed in modern style crept in and tried to go up the stairs obviously without being heard.

"Is that you?" The voice was slurred but held the menace familiar to the pack.

"Y-yes Dad."

"Well get your idle arse in here and get me some grub."

Visibly trembling she slowly moved towards the kitchen. She'd tried many times to make it habitable but every time she did he would come home in a drunken rage and throw things about not caring about the mess or what he smashed in the process. By now she was close to breaking point, losing all interest in the house, her father, or anything to do with him.

"What the hell are you doing?" The voice boomed again.

"Going to do some toast." It was the first thing that came into her mind before he had chance to yell again, but she knew the place wasn't fit to do any kind of food. She lived on packet snacks or takeaways. Unbeknown to him she had a small part time job which provided her food and clothes, but if she had told him about it he would have taken her money for his drink so she just said she was out with friends.

The tirade which came out of his mouth was unrepeatable as he called her into the room, ordering her to cook him a proper meal. She came in slowly, and within seconds he had grabbed her and was shaking her, the smell of his breath making her heave. The dogs were on standby and this was the trigger point.

Tisun had already located the nearest police car and was running in the road in full view of the driver who was on his radio that a beautiful red setter was running though the traffic, and was obviously a pedigree that must have escaped. Another car responded as back up. The dog was drawing the police car nearer and nearer to the house and when he was level with it, the officer watched amazed as Tisun turned and stood on his hind legs at the front window. As the house had no front garden, the window was easily accessible as it looked directly onto the pavement. Another police vehicle arrived and the officer got out, automatically switching on his body cam.

"Look" the first man said pointing at the house but looking at his colleague.

"My God." His colleague was on the radio immediately to control to report what he was seeing, at the same time gesticulating for the other one to get inside. But he wasn't reporting seeing a dog, red setter or any other image that Tisun may have chosen. If he was amazed, it was nothing to what the first man felt for there in full view was the father holding his daughter by the throat as she pounded him with blows but due to her slight frame she stood little chance against his drink powered strength.

"No! No! You promised you wouldn't." she was screaming but this had no effect.

He was ripping her top then groping at her breasts, drooling over them. He released one of his arms and grabbed her free hand ramming it down to his crotch.

She screamed hysterically "Not again." Then she struggled with all her strength but she could feel the energy going.

Fortunately she liked the current fashion of leggings or tights worn under a pair of denim shorts and this was to her advantage now as he tried to pull them down but as that was difficult, tried to get his hand up one of the legs and even that was impossible. It had been much easier when he had caught her in her nightwear many times and now his anger was taking over at the frustration which was building up at the top of his legs.

With a feeble cry of "Help" it was as though her prayer was answered for the first PC burst in through the door, followed by the other who had been filming everything from the other side of the window. The officers ripped the man away leaving the girl in a heap on the floor, exhausted.

At times like this there was no rule book, they had to restrain him whatever it took, and they certainly did. They were both married with children of their own and the thought that a father could do this to one of his own sickened them and they had no mercy for they felt he deserved none.

Other officers arrived shortly after, some to remove the man in a vehicle more suitable to his condition and also a family liaison officer to take over the future care of the girl. Hopefully her torment was over although they all knew that if this had been going on for some time, maybe years, recovery wouldn't happen that quickly...

The dogs had excelled themselves although to them it was just routine work. While Tisun had led official help right to the door the two beagles had drawn the man towards the window and at the right moment, used their kinetic skills to pull back the curtains thus allowing him to be caught in the act. Tisun had already made sure the door was not locked so the police would have immediate access. The timing had been perfect and as their job was complete they all returned to base.

Some time later the first two officers on the scene would be writing their reports and the subject of the dòg would be raised. One had definitely seen it but it seemed to vanish when the other arrived. They decided that if it was still at large it would be caught and if micro chipped could be traced back to its owner. They both felt it best not to mention that one had seen it standing on its hind legs at the window whilst the other didn't. There were some things better not reported for fear the officer's efficiency might be jeopardised. It would be treated like a UFO sighting, no proof so why stir the waters?

The rest of the pack were always pleased when a job was dealt with quickly, as were most assignments but some took every bit of skill and mental cunning they could muster. At such times the whole group needed to be free and if minor jobs came in they could sometimes allocate them to the standby spirit dogs. But until they had more facts about the possible warehouse situation they had to perform as normal.

Recently there had been a spate of various kinds of bullying, some physically terrifying, but some were more of the mental torment variety. Although Tisun was glad the last job had achieved the possibility of a brighter future for the victim, the reports being received now were of a much deeper level and may take time to get control of them.

Many children get bullied at school, but not all are obvious. The taunting can be annoying but if the child shows no interest, the offender often gets fed up and chooses someone else. The case now facing the lads seemed to be a simple one and should be sorted without any hassle so Mildew opted to go before he was called for his earth duty.

The girls school was fairly large with pupils aged eleven onwards.

"Hmm, case of larger ones picking on the newcomers I expect," Mildew had seen a lot of this kind of thing, resulting in the young ones growing and then taking it out on ones smaller than themselves. A bit of an annoyance at the time, but it was when things went further the trouble started. His nose led him to the girl at the centre of this report. Her own bitch, Dinky guarded her unseen and was upset by the happenings, but was not experienced enough to sort it, so she contacted the pack.

Mildew greeted her and she pointed out her friend Hannah. At first he thought there must be a mistake, this girl looked more like a bully herself but Dinky assured him it was a living hell so asked him to be patient and watch.

The bell went for the girls to go into school and there was a mad rush to get through the doors and along the corridors. Mildew instinctively stepped back as though he thought he was going to be trampled in the chaos.

"Watch this" Dinky pulled him to where Hannah was about to go into her classroom. One of the other girls purposely jostled her so that she was pushed against another girl whose books fell to the floor.

"I saw that Preston. Apologise to her, pick up her books and see me in the staffroom in break." The teacher's voice boomed over the fracas.

"That was a set up," Mildew observed, "but why?"

"But that's only part of it."

"Has she ever done anything to upset them, got them into trouble for instance?"

Dinky shook her head. "Nothing. She was always popular then suddenly this teacher came and seems to have it in for her, but it's beyond me."

Mildew asked, "So if it stems from the teacher, why would the other girls be part of it?"

"That's what I was hoping you could find out." Dinky said coyly. She liked the power of this dog and wished he could be there all the time.

"Right, lets have a closer look at this teacher."

"Good, she's taking Hannah's class right now, so you will see."

The two were in the room instantly and if she could have seen the dog watching her every move, this teacher would have been terrified, for she was afraid of dogs.

"Ah, that may have something to do with it." Mildew was picking up something and said "Could you go out into the corridor for a moment please?"

Dinky would have stood on her head for him but did as she was asked. Mildew watched the woman carefully. He noticed her eyes always came back to Hannah, not just now and again but almost alternately. She would speak to the class, return, pick out one of the girls to answer a question, return and this was continual, so she had a fixation of some sort. Either she picked up the continual presence of Dinky, or she had some sort of hatred fixation for Hannah. Nothing seemed to have changed so Mildew called Dinky back.

"Well?" she asked.

"Just testing a theory, probably nothing." was all he would offer. Then said "Would you mind watching for a moment. Thank you."

She was amazed he hadn't even waited for a reply, but he obviously knew what he was doing and she was pleased to have him here more and more every minute. The teacher carried on almost ignoring Hannah when it came to answering questions but still returned to her as if she were a focal point. Mildew had passed this observation on to Dinky without her realising it, but now she became fascinated watching this particular habit. Why hadn't she noticed it before? Then it came to her. Up to now her attention had been more on her friend so she wouldn't have been watching the teacher, but this was enlightening.

Mildew returned and Dinky couldn't wait to tell him what she had discovered but it was met with the merest of acknowledgments. "Maybe train her yet." He thought.

It crossed his mind that he could already put a stop to all of this with a few simple tricks of his own, but he was curious to know what was at the bottom of it, and he may just force some of the players to react and see what followed. But first he must see how the woman treated the girl during the break, although for now it wouldn't hurt to have a bit of fun.

The teacher turned to pick up a book from her desk but Mildew gave it a slight push and it fell to the floor. As she retrieved it and stood up her face went a deep shade of pink which made a few of the girls start to snigger.

"Bet she farted when she bent over." One whispered to her friend but more heard this than she expected and soon the whole class were trying to suppress their giggles. Mildew had stage managed this for a reason and now he was searching to see which girls didn't show they found it amusing for they would be the ones under her thumb for whatever reason. There were two, one at the front and one at the back who were in agony trying not to laugh but knew better of it for the teacher was watching them like a hawk. For once her attention seemed to be away from Hannah, but suddenly she swung round pointing at her.

"It's all your fault. Now you will be punished."

That seemed to quieten the atmosphere for every girl in the room knew she had nothing to do with it. It was time for another test. Slowly Mildew pushed Hannah up until she was in a standing position.

"And what was I suppose to have done Miss? Please tell me."

The whole room froze in amazement, not only because of the apparent cheek of standing up to the woman but the calmness with which the words came out like bullets.

" I-I - you know very well." she stuttered.

"If I knew that Miss, I wouldn't need to ask." Hannah stood her ground her eyes fixed.

The bell sounded for break and usually the whole class would have left the room as though their only object in life was to be first through the door. A plague of locusts couldn't have come close to the operation. But now all were perfectly still.

"Well Miss, if that's all, perhaps you will excuse me. I have an appointment in the staffroom if you remember."

The teacher couldn't compose herself or understand what had just happened and muttered "Oh not now, I've got more important things to worry about." and hurried out as if her life depended on it. Hannah gave a satisfied little nod and collected her books. It was the only time that the rest of the class let her leave first.

"You did that." Dinky was jumping up and down.

"What?" Mildew was appearing to concentrate on something else.

"Whatever it was, you did it, I know you did it."

Ignoring her he asked "Where is your body right now?"

"Oh I'm asleep on my bed. Her parents go out to work so I won't be disturbed until lunchtime when I'm let out."

"Then what about the afternoon?"

"On my own again, well the cat comes in and out of the cat flap, so I'm not really alone, but there's no people, or any other dogs. I'm the only dog."

Mildew was beginning to wish he'd never asked

"So you are here in the afternoon as well?" He managed to stem the flow.

"Oh yes, every day, well school days, there wouldn't be any point in my being here at weekends, there's no school then."

If he could have put a paw over her mouth he would have been very tempted, but knew he could probably use this lively little soul as she adored Hannah and the love would come in useful at the right moment.

"Well, I may be around for a bit but let's get one thing straight."

"Oh anything you say, I just want Hannah to be left alone and not picked on."

"Right. Well if I tell you, sorry, ask you to do something, no matter how strange it may seem, will you do it?"

"Well, I think I could. What kind of thing?"

"You will find out when the time comes. It may be simple like just watching someone for me. Think you are up to it?"

Dinky had taken quite a liking to this big powerful dog and the thought of being near him for a while was quite exciting.

"I'll do anything you say."

"Thank goodness," he thought but said "Fine. I am leaving you now, just carry on as normal but remember anything you feel might be important."

She was about to ask what could be important but he had gone before her spiritual jaw was open.

Mildew soon contacted Tisun for an update but it was a distance talk as the need was felt for him to stay around the school area.

"Something's not adding up, in fact none of it makes sense."

"Elaborate." Tisun wanted him to get to the point.

"Everything. But I want to do a few tests before I'm sure on some points."

"Such as?"

"Well, the teacher, a Miss Clemence, doesn't like dogs and was very uncomfortable when I was in the room. Wonder if Dinky's presence is why she picks on Hannah, but without realising it. I need to know if she can see us or feels us being there."

Tisun was silent for a moment. "But you said there are two girls involved in the bullying. What about the rest of the class?"

"Just get on with their own work mostly, but don't think they'd like to fall out with the other two, and they detest the teacher."

"Doesn't sound too serious but we can never be sure. Keep me posted." and he was gone.

Mildew was a very distrusting dog and never took anything at face value. He would sit and reflect upon recent happenings, a process which had often turned out to be to his advantage. He would sift and resift the knowledge obtained and often a tiny fragment would alert his senses and would prove to be the missing link. His mind turned to Dinky. Why would such a simple little thing contact the pack directly? She was obviously very spiritually aware and would know she had to go through the normal channels to request assistance. There was a vetting system which passed minor problems to other workers and only the more severe messages reached the pack. So when a hoax call came in, there was a good chance it wasn't merely a trouble maker but came from a more sinister source. Again the question. Why would a seemingly innocent little mongrel want them to protect her friend from bullying when she was in a position to deal with it herself? She had the teacher's fear of dogs on her side so she could easily use that weapon. There had to be something deeper and he must detect it and soon.

Miss Clemence was making her way to her next class and Mildew stood in her way blocking her path. She halted abruptly and stood frozen to the spot. He moved to her side, then behind her watching to see if her eyes followed him but she kept staring straight ahead. He pulled back and she continued to walk, so he moved to her side and she stopped again but didn't look in his direction. Now he knew, she couldn't see him but knew when he was near, so she was spiritually aware but by how much? That would be the next test.

The two bullies were in the toilet block being watched by Dinky. At a given point she pushed one against the other until they were face to face leaning against the wall. At that moment a girl breezed in and stopped in faked amazement. Her mane of bright red hair was so magnificent, she would stand out in a crowd.

27

"Well, well," she mocked, "so that's the way it is with you two."
The two parted but moved to flank her on each side.
"Don't be stupid." one spat at her.
"Are you trying to say we're a couple of dykes?" the other added.
The red head laughed and pushed them away. "Oh I'm not trying to say anything. I only know what I saw, but I guess the others will find it amusing," then turning to face them, narrowed her eyes and added "or disgusting."

"Wait a minute. We don't know you. Are you new here?" The first one asked.
"Yeah, new." her friend sounding like an echo, backed her up.
"Let's get her."
"Yeah, let's get her."

As the two faced her, she fixed them with a steady gaze, her form changing to that of a grey wolf, eyes blazing and the teeth drawing nearer by the second. They were at a loss as to what to do, gasping in fright and trying to call for help but the words stuck in their throats.

As quickly as it had started, all had returned to normal except both were crying with fear. The red head looked them up and down then left with the retort "Suggest you change your underwear ladies."

Mildew had sensed the interchange and was observing from a distance. Perhaps some of his work was being done for him, but for now he would keep his distance as he didn't want to lose any vital points by showing his hand, but he would certainly keep this newcomer in view. Obviously she was there for a reason and he felt it wasn't only to sift out the bullies.

He decided to follow Dinky's route at lunchtime just to be sure she was on the level. Although he had tried to do a trace earlier, he couldn't seem to pick up the spiritual path she should have left when she came with Hannah that morning. If she was using a body there could have been some sort of trace as the physical disturbed the surroundings in such a way that it took longer to settle then when just a spirit passed. That would have made things easier but according to the dog she left her earthly form on her bed so would only have travelled in spirit. He mulled this over a few times but an instinct told him all was not as it seemed.

Now he had a hunch. Toning up his senses he went off on a tour of the school concentrating on all Hannah's class members and any other teachers they had. He homed in on one very quiet girl who seemed to keep away from the crowd, but never got taunted. In fact one could almost forget she was there most of the time. She never seemed to be in the surge rushing in and out of the rooms, yet was always ready at her desk when class began. His spiritual nose was now working overtime. She was on her way to the next class when she suddenly stopped dead and pretended to read a notice board. It was a guess as to who was the most surprised.

"Who are you?" she thought.

"I could ask you the same." Mildew was standing at her side.

"Keep away from me, you'll spoil everything."

"Might be able to help. What are you doing?"

"Go away."

"Oh, undercover are we?"

As her persistence didn't pay off, she turned and walked away, but he was after her.

"I will be at your side until you tell me, or I find out." He was adamant.

"You don't understand, now please."

"Ok have it your way." And he was gone.

She breathed a sigh of relief but knew he would be watching her every move in some way or another.

The pack was wondering where their colleague had got to. They had dealt with many bullying cases and it seemed to be on the increase, but they didn't always require the dog to be in constant presence, which meant they knew Mildew certainly had his teeth into something and wouldn't let go until he had unearthed the truth, which in his line was very apt.

"Wonder what he's up to."

"Hope they don't recall him before he's finished."

"He could still work on it."

"Not if it's going to be a long one."

Tisun listened to the thought waves then cut in "OK, he's clever enough to root out anything if its there so lets wait. Agreed?"

They all had no option but secretly hoped that if there was something juicy going on he may need their help. Little did they realise what his next communication would reveal.

Chapter 3

A covert watch was being kept on the warehouse, although the pack was careful not to make it too obvious by going themselves. Several of the support helpers who had higher levels of detection were seconded on a one off basis, to report then stay well away. Radar being in the vicinity was not going to be used this time as it seemed safer to bring in workers from further afield.

It was obvious that the area was being used for some purpose and was either being vetted by an alien or spiritual force, or it had already been selected and was being prepared for whatever operation was being planned. The latest news was that the footprints were increasing. They were not only in the air but were covering the building inside and out like a protective shield. Another strange feature was that there was an unbroken line of them around the warehouse but not touching it, almost like a protective moat round a castle. Further reports proved the prints were all of the same kind so were probably multi purpose, forming a shield but also acting as a detection of unwelcome visitors.

Tisun was anxious to know how far this force extended, in other words what was a safe distance, commonly referred to as 'the last dead cow', but sensibly the helpers hadn't ventured near enough to find out. There was also the fact that they didn't know if this would act against physical attacks or just spiritual ones, but maybe both. There was only one way to find out.

The dogs were restless. Surely the leader wasn't going to send in a person in the bodily state, as that would be sadistic. But he had an idea which may seem unsavoury to some but could avert a major attack later. They would have to be a little patient but the main thing was to keep continual observations on the place. In his wisdom Tisun knew it wouldn't be that long before he had his answer but didn't explain further at this point.

Mildew made an unexpected appearance and asked for a recap of the footprints upon which he announced that he had traced similar deposits at the school, although these were more like handprints, but with the thumb missing. This caused deep concern and raised the question as to whether that was the real reason for summoning the pack, and had nothing to do with bullying. When they had reacted to the news he dropped his next bombshell.

The pack, although probably the best, wasn't the only such group of vigilantes operating on the spiritual level. The 'Ladydogs' had been in presence for some time trying to combat the spate of concentrated bullying at various schools in the area. Their group, made up of entirely females, put their success down to giving the impression of just playing at their job resulting in the opposition treating them as a bit of a laugh, but then having one almighty shock when they struck.

Dinky, as he suspected wasn't the chattering airhead she portrayed, and was working along with 'Redhead' and the quiet girl. Hannah although due to be on one of her refresher courses in body, was also a member and had been placed in the position of being the butt of Miss Clemence's attention.

Imagine their frustration when Mildew appeared on the scene just as they were about to launch their attack to root out all the perpetrators and scare the hell out of them. Redhead had also noticed the hand prints but not knowing what they were had dismissed them for the time being. So it didn't suit the pack's plan for the ladies to stir it up just now when it seemed there could be a connection to the warehouse and whatever locations were involved.

Tisun returned with Mildew and located Redhead who called the others to her. He explained that they had a much bigger operation going on and that the Ladydogs were in danger of jeopardising it and would they kindly carry on as normal so as not to raise any suspicion, except that he didn't put it quite as politely as that! They got the message, and although didn't quite appreciate his manners, realised there had to be good reason for his bluntness. Begrudgingly they agreed but secretly looked forward to having a grandstand seat when it all kicked off. There was no mention of the prints as he didn't want the females sniffing round and arousing interest from any other source. With that both male dogs returned to base.

A few minor jobs had come in which were dealt with by the rest of the pack, but they still had their senses on full alert for anything out of the ordinary, no matter where they were located at the time for the tiniest thing could hold a clue.

Suddenly, Tisun's hackles went up and he called them all to task.

"Here we go." he said as he indicated for them to spread out around the warehouse, but keeping at different distances from it. They could even keep changing positions to avoid being monitored.

It was late afternoon with light rain falling and visibility wasn't that good from an earthly view but the dogs had clear sense of the man approaching the building. He walked along the boundary of the premises pulling at the high wire fencing. When he got to one point, he bent down and pulled the fence up from the ground and crawled under. Judging by the ground it was something he had done several times before.

"Now watch closely." Tisun warned, positioning himself directly behind the object of attention.

"It's just an old tramp." Blue thought but knew better than to dismiss the appearance.

It appeared to all watching that this gentleman of the road was looking for some shelter from the elements, but he seemed to know just where he was going so it must be a regular place where he could get some sleep or just rest for a while.

All the dogs were now so much on alert that their spiritual hair was standing on end in anticipation. The man shuffled forward then stopped. He looked around as if to see if he was being watched, then to their relief started moving towards one of the doors at the side of the building. He was only about two yards away when he fell to the ground and remained motionless as his soul was slowly released from the dejected body and his days of hardship were at an end. But it wasn't time for sentiment and Tisun called the dogs back to base.

So now they had their 'last dead cow' line and it coincided with the footprints forming the 'moat' which meant that anywhere up to there was safe for now in the earthly sense. This made the lads look up.

"Only earthly?" King wanted to know. "Could it extend further for spirit?"

"Can't be sure, which means we still have to be diligent, but one thing is certain, we do not venture to take any looks inside however brief, we do not do any sweeps over it unless from a great distance and..." Tisun paused "we don't use any helpers from now on. Understood?"

Noodle had been very quiet which hadn't gone unnoticed.

"We know what's bothering you." Mildew nudged him.

"Voice it. Get it out of your thoughts." Tisun ordered quite sharply.

After a moment the Beagle said "I know you didn't send him but you knew that tramp was going to go there didn't you?"

"Of course."

"And you let him be used as a guinea pig." The dog looked sad.

"Depends how you look at it. I actually did him a favour."

They all turned at that so Tisun explained.

"Been watching him for a while. Wasn't always like that you know. Just gone downhill rapidly, had a lot of sadness. He was constantly praying for the Lord to take him so he could be with his wife."

"You knew he wouldn't survive whatever is out there." Mildew stated.

"Poor man." Noodle still felt for him.

"Oh don't waste your pity, he'll be fine as soon as he's gone through his transition." Then said "See for yourself."

All dogs turned to the direction he was indicating and Noodle's tail was waving in delight for they could see the wife waiting with arms outstretched while the tramp image slipped away and the most handsome man emerged to join her.

"Still miserable?" Tisun asked.

"Oh no, he's so happy now." Noodles tail was wagging at full pace but the leader pulled their attention back to the problem in hand.

"There has to be a connection with that school and who knows how many other places." Tisun was serious now." Take that as a lesson. If that can happen at that place, think what could happen at others."

The truth dawned. If the prints were that lethal, schoolchildren could be at risk, or hospitals, or anywhere where they were traced. Something had to be done soon, but with the utmost caution for this was a situation the pack had never faced before.

Hannah had been advised to revert back to her meeker self and force Miss Clemence's hand. The dogs would take it in turn to be in presence but asked the Ladydogs not to communicate with them unless requested. They didn't take kindly to that as they weren't used to taking orders from outside, but knew they had no option as they too sensed there was more afoot.

King was on duty and was trying to form a pattern made by the hand prints, but like the warehouse they didn't seem to conform to any order and were dotted about all over the building, but didn't seem to be in the grounds at all. He formed a chart in his mind. There were several in the gym, a few in the kitchen, the odd one or two in the toilets, one here and there in the corridors and classrooms and quite a lot in the staffroom. Now that seemed odd. Next he examined the outside walls of the building but they were completely clean. He was looking for a similarity to the warehouse and glad no moat like footprints were to be found.

An idea came to him. He took a mental image of one of the prints nearest to him then returned to base and compared it with the images they had of the others. What he found made them all sit up in amazement. There was a distinct difference and he blamed himself for not having noticed it before. For some reason they were opposite, that is the warehouse were concave, whilst the school one was convex. In an instant he returned to the school and examined the others and they were all the same. But why? Also they urgently needed to know the whereabouts of any more, not only to be prepared but to see if they were any different to the two already discovered.

This appeared to be a mammoth task but suddenly Tisun came up with a plan so simple, but at the same time exceedingly dangerous.

Clemence was in the staff room. It was dinner time and other teachers were either busy overseeing the meals or deep in discussion with matters she found mundane. She needed time to think and sort out her mind and although didn't have to explain her self to anyone, said in passing that she had to nip out to the shops. From experience she had learned that if you give people enough information they tend not to ask questions and don't give it a second thought as to where you might be.

She sat in her car going over the events of the morning. It had really thrown her when Hannah answered her back. What had made the girl do it? Plus the overwhelming feeling that there was a distinct dog presence in the atmosphere which seemed to be getting stronger by the moment. Surely this had something to do with the Hannah girl as she had never noticed it before. It was too much of a coincidence to be otherwise. Well she had better up the pressure.

As soon as she had returned to the building she located her two bullies and gave them a sign to go into action which was met with utter delight as they knew they could get away with almost anything without being punished. They soon located their prey outside and positioned themselves either side of her. One nudged her, gently at first, followed by the other until the force almost knocked her over. They hooted with laughter as she regained her balance. The temptation to react was so strong but she knew she must take the taunts in order to get to the bottom of the Clemence involvement.

"Bet you made her mad," one jeered "do it again, give us a laugh."

"Yeah go on, do it again." her echo added.

Hannah stood before them in silence.

"Ha, she's too scared, might get into trouble."

"She's scared."

"Dare you."

Hannah started to move forward between the two of them.

"And give you all something to laugh at. Pity you have such small minds."

"Ooooh, get her. Aren't we the brave one?" They both started to push her again and with the jibes in her ears, she kicked backward with her foot catching the underdog hard on her shin which caused her to fall down clutching at her leg screaming in pain. Hannah turned and smiled then walked off.

"Now you've done it you bitch." The chief bully yelled after her as she bent down to her mate.

"I certainly am," thought Hannah wishing she could wave her tail in deviance.

By the beginning of the afternoon session, Hannah had been summoned to the head's office to explain her actions. Clemence

35

stood there rubbing her hands knowing the girl couldn't wriggle out of this one.

"So how do you explain yourself for this vicious attack?" The head looked stern.

Hannah look confused then asked "Which attack please miss?"

"No don't be clever girl, you know perfectly well which one. What have you got to say?"

The teachers had no idea that Redhead and Dinky had joined them and were studying Clemence at close range. Hannah suppressed the amusement and looking the head straight in the eye said "Well if you mean when the two girls from my class assaulted me from both sides without provocation, I would think it is they who should be answering this question."

The dogs moved nearer to Clemence and started licking her legs which made her rub her hands all the more vigorously which was now very noticeable. Hannah stood with her head on one side waiting for a reply.

"And did this happen before you caused injury to one of them?" The head asked.

"Did I? Oh it must have been when I was trying to pull away, I didn't look back but heard one of them shout."

There was a pause while the head looked from one to the other before saying "Well you know we don't tolerate unruly behaviour and girls of your age should know better. You may go now but I suggest you keep your distance from them in future." The look she gave her wasn't unkind and as Hannah started to leave, Clemence started to follow her but was stopped.

"Just a minute Miss Clemence, could you spare a moment please?"

The woman looked shocked as she couldn't get out of the room quick enough, partly to give the girl a mouthful, but partly to escape this horrible feeling that was crawling over her whole body.

"Do you want to stay?" Redhead asked.

"Rather," Dinky replied, "guess we've got her on the run, anyway, wouldn't want to miss the fun." The two stood either side of their plaything.

"Now then, did you know all about this before you brought the girl to me?"

"But you don't know what she's like. Oh she may seem like butter wouldn't melt but I can tell you I've seen a completely different side. An insolent side and if you'll pardon my saying so, I think she has been let off lightly. I would have punished her."

Her senior eyed her up. "Do you need the toilet?"

"No, no, why should you ask that?"

The dogs were almost crying with amusement.

"Wish we were males, we could have peed up her legs."

"Stop it."

The head continued "Well you seem to be hopping about, keep still."

"I'm sorry but it seems so unfair."

There was an uncomfortable pause before the reply came.

"Well Miss Clemence it depends upon what you call unfair. You see I happen to know that what the girl said was all perfectly true. She was taunted, pushed, goaded, and if others had been in her position they would have landed out and given one of them a black eye or worse."

The dogs moved in until they were squashing the woman's legs giving her the sensation of what it feels like to be trapped.

"Well... I mean... how can you believe what she says? She's a liar as well, I expect." Clemence was stuttering now and clutching at straws.

"Because I saw it."

"What?"

"I happened to be looking out of my window. It overlooks the part at the side that isn't usually very busy so anyone there stands out. How Hannah kept her cool I will never know, and yes, as she tried to move forward her leg shot back and caught one of the others, and let me tell you that if she hadn't they would still be annoying her now."

The dogs gave each other a knowing sign and left, Dinky quickly returning to Hannah to share the news. They couldn't fathom what role this teacher played but felt she wasn't just being a tyrant for the sake of power and needed to keep a close watch on her until they knew.

Miss Clemence made her way to the staff washroom as slowly as she could to freshen up. She didn't want to attract attention by

37

hurrying although she couldn't get there quick enough. There was no uncomfortable presence here and she began to doubt her sanity, seriously wondering if she was imagining the whole thing. But she would soon find out and definitely wish she hadn't.

King had witnessed all this and returned to base where only Tisun and Mildew were present, the others all being out on jobs. An interesting fact had occurred. While the bullying session and the meeting with the head had been going on, the handprints had increased noticeably. Tisun quickly did a distance scan of the warehouse to check on any change in the footprints there but they seemed to be exactly the same, but he believed that they had all been placed, and that side of the protection was complete ready for the main operation, whereas the school was still being set up. They desperately needed to know of any other building where either of the prints may start appearing but at present these seemed to be the only two. It was time for Tisun to put his scheme into operation but he would only get one shot at it.

It would be difficult to describe the many ways in which the spirit world works, especially when dealing with such unknown skills often used by the ultimate powers. However, in simple terms Tisun was going to visit the school and take an image of one of the convex handprints at close range then project it, vaguely similar to a hologram, in waste land well away from any habited area. Then he and he alone would monitor the print using some of his own skills, at least this is what he told the pack just before he set off. If he had been honest with them, there is no way they would have let him undertake such a dangerous mission.

His reasoning was that whatever was planting the prints would wonder why one had gone astray and reposition it, either at the school or elsewhere. But he wasn't confining it to one, he was going to scatter them all over England and see where they ended up. But that wasn't all. He would not be observing them from above, he would be inside the images, splitting his being into as many parts as were required. Knowing how destructive the concave footprints were to the physical, and not being able to test them on the spiritual, he had opted for the convex hand variety in the hope that while they were not en masse, they would not be lethal, but this was only conjecture. The risk had to be taken and he would not send anyone else to do it. He now took time alone to prepare himself and hone the skills he needed for this to be a success.

Redhead had decided to work on Clemence full time.

"I'll break her." she smirked. It always amused the others when she did this in her spirit form for she used a Dalmatian trait of lifting one lip up to show her teeth as if grinning. Whatever breed she had occupied during her earth visits, she kept this going and it became her trademark.

"Don't think it'll take much now" Dinky was remembering the office scene.

"She's not the strong character she'd like to be" Hannah said, "bit sad really."

"Which makes me wonder." The quiet girl had been taking all this in.

"Yes?" was the chorus.

"If she is the pawn."

"Could be." they agreed, but Redhead wanted her to elaborate.

"I've been watching her closely. When she is away from the school she seems a timid sad little thing, so is all this an act, or does she have some sort of inferiority complex and has to take it out on the easiest target?"

"Agreed," Dinky said "but that doesn't explain why she has her two satellites doing half the work. Surely she would get the buzz from making someone's life a misery by her own hand."

"Power." Redhead stated. "She'll probably enlist more as time goes on, let's stop her now, won't be difficult."

"Then she will need the toilet." Hannah wished she had seen that earlier scene.

King had been homing in on this conversation and on returning to base expressed his concern.

"This pack is drawing too much attention to the place. They could jeopardise our operation if we aren't careful."

"Maybe not." Blue had been thinking. "Couldn't it draw attention just to the bullying while we get on with our job and take the attention off us instead?"

39

"Still a bit risky." King felt.

Tisun took charge. "There are both points of view, and at present we still don't know exactly what is going on with Clemence so we will let them carry on or it may look suspicious."

"Plus the fact those feisty little girls wouldn't be told." King added.

"Exactly." Tisun wasn't wasting words as it was time for him to go into action.

One of Jack's dog handler colleagues had come to take him and Radar where the dog could have a good exercise for although his master was making a good recovery, he had to be careful how he used his arm at present.

They were in the friend's own estate car which had a dog gate at the back so Radar had a 360 degree view of everything as opposed to the police dog vans. Out of consideration, the man took a slight detour so that he didn't drive past the warehouse but the road was near enough for Radar to be able to home in on it without appearing to be having it under observation, as Tisun's ruling had been passed on to all concerned. Although he was out of visual range, he had a clear spiritual view of the place. In horror he noticed two cats chasing a loose piece of paper around in the breeze but it was taking them nearer to the print perimeter by the second. He was about to send out a warning vibe when the paper hit what appeared to be an invisible wall and the cats took the opportunity to jump after it but fell back to the ground bewildered, although completely unharmed. He watched as they approached with caution but again drew back when they came up against something they could feel but not see. This was enough for them and they crept away, glancing behind them their back fur standing on end. When they reached a gap in the fence they hurried through and shot off to wherever they lived.

Radar breathed a sigh of relief but suddenly realised what the driver was saying to Jack.

"Oh by the way, that old tramp I told you about that was found dead at the warehouse, well seems he died of a heart attack, could have happened at any time."

"Poor old beggar," Jack mused "to have to die like that, all alone."

As they continued talking, Radar knew that as soon as Jack was asleep he must bring him up to speed, but for now he sent the very important message back to the pack, where they jumped on this new revelation.

"So the boundary isn't lethal," Tisun paused in his preparations, "it's only a force field."

"Still need to know why." Blue said.

"We do, but it alters the whole situation. Whatever it is wants to keep everything out, but doesn't appear to have set up any other defence."

"When do we find out?" King wondered.

"We – don't." Tisun was adamant. "It is too much an unknown factor. If we send one of us in possibly to their spiritual destruction, who would we choose? We can't sent a helper in for two reasons, one they wouldn't be knowledgeable enough and two we could be sending an innocent soul to their doom. If on the other hand we went as a pack, we could all be destroyed."

This quietened them all and before anyone else could come up with a suggestion Tisun said "Leave it for now. I may find the answer from the other source."

"Oh, when you lay your image traps?" was the general hum of agreement.

"Exactly. Now I have to get that into operation."

If the others knew what their leader had in mind they may not have settled so easily.

Their time was never boring and they received a request for help regarding an employee whose owner was accusing him of theft which he knew was totally unfounded and felt he was being victimised. This was a job Fleece could handle on his own and it didn't usually take long for him to get a satisfactory result. He hovered over the small petrol station just outside of a small town in Norfolk. The cashier was making a 'drop' of cash as he approached. The till was set to give a warning when a certain level, in this case two hundred pounds was reached and the amount was rung out, placed in a canister and put down a chute which went directly into the security office, which when the manager wasn't there was locked, so there was no way any drop could be retrieved after it had been deposited.

The cashier always recorded the canister number onto his work sheet so that the whole shift could be balanced. The manager had accused him on two occasions of there being a drop missing, making a total of four hundred pounds short which he threatened to take out of the man's wages. This caused an argument, with the cashier telling him that not only was it illegal, but the amount was a lot to him and although he didn't say it, wondered why the boss didn't sack him if he believed he was stealing. The spirit guarding the employee knew the manager was taking the money himself and blaming the staff member, and if he sacked him, who would be blamed? The young spirit didn't know how he could prove it and had requested help from the pack.

Fleece's first question was "Was any other cashier also being accused?"

"No," was the answer "only this man."

"Then that seems strange."

The spirit looked puzzled so Fleece explained. "It is such a small amount by some standards. If he needed money surely he would be looking for much more."

He decided to monitor the situation thoroughly, and luckily the same cashier was on duty for the next three nights.

"Here's what we will do." He explained, checking the till area. "With a little nudge from us, get the man to show his canister to the camera, put the notes with the slip inside, always on full view then stand well back so that he is in seen clearly when he drops it through the hatch. Then you can go with him when he goes off duty, and I will be here to watch the boss empty the floor safe."

The young spirit seemed pleased to have someone experienced on his side and was sensible enough to learn a few of the tricks at the same time.

They both watched the man through the night. He seemed very diligent, locking the shop door at a certain time and then serving through the night hatch, stocking the shelves and cleaning the food area. When the morning papers arrived he checked them in and got ready to balance his shift as soon his relief arrived a quarter of an hour early to give him chance to run his till report and get off on time.

All seemed well in order and Fleece couldn't help but imagine the poor man's face if he knew how closely guarded he had been when he thought he was completely alone. Bidding farewell to his spirit companion he watched the day cashier fill out his sheet, check the change bags and do all the little bits that went to having everything to hand so that the job ran efficiently. They all had their own little foibles, liking certain things in special places to suit their own choice.

It was nine o'clock before the manager arrived and after making a coffee settled down to checking the sheets from the previous twenty four hours. He unlocked the safe, lifted out the canisters and put them in a row in front of him. Fleece was aware of a certain smell when the man was there but it hadn't been there all night. Quickly he asked for Noodle to join him.

"I know the smell, what is it?" he asked him.

It only took one sniff for his mate to say "Salted nuts, cashews to be precise."

"Of course, many thanks."

"Any time." Noodle nodded and was gone.

Fleece hovered around the office while the canisters were emptied, not only onto the desk area to be counted but, after checking on the sheets which ones had been dropped on the nightshift, the contents of two found their way into his pocket. Now all that Fleece had to do was provide the evidence to prove the cashier was not to blame. First he located the young spirit and told him of his plans, then he contacted a local police officer nearing retirement but with a 'nose' for delving into cases and finding things others had missed. In fact he was very spiritually tuned although in his waking life just put it down to intuition.

There was no option but to play the waiting game through the day so Fleece returned to base to catch up with the rest of the pack that were available then returned to the station. The manager was waiting for the night cashier to arrive and met him with the accusation that he was short on two drops, and that if he did it again he would be sacked. The cashier started to say that he could prove he had dropped the money but Fleece was steering the boss to the door as the young spirit closed the employee's mouth, rendering him speechless.

Having got the true thief out of the way, Fleece now homed in on the constable, having already checked he would be on duty at that time. The officer was driving his car towards the station when the thought came into his mind to call in. Ideas were flying round his brain, and he felt he must ask a few questions, but he decided to leave it until later as it was very busy now and not the right time for getting anyone's attention.

Some time later, after he had taken his break he pulled onto the forecourt and went into the shop area. After the first pleasantries he stood by the counter casually chatting to the cashier, although the words were being fed to him, as would the responses be.

"You had any problems here lately lad?"

"Umm not really. Been lucky I suppose."

The officer looked him straight in the eye. "Only I heard there's a bit of thieving going on."

"Oh, oh, really, well I don't think we've noticed anything."

"Are you sure? You can tell me, like you know if anything was troubling you."

The cashier felt as though this man already knew, but wondered how. Then it occurred to him.

"Why? What's he said?"

"What's who said?" The gaze was steady and enquiring. After a slight pause he continued "Why don't you tell me from your side of things?"

"You know?"

"When did it start?" The officer knew his instinct hadn't let him down. Now all he had to do was find out what was going on.

"Not sure exactly, recently though." The cashier suddenly wondered if he was walking into a trap. "Hey, you're not going to arrest me are you if I tell you?"

"Let's take one step at a time shall we? Now then, you were saying."

Slowly Fleece guided the man through the accusations and explained that he had recorded the drops on his sheet and even shown them to the camera.

"Now what made you do that?"

44

"Well he was saying I hadn't dropped the cash and I know I had so I thought the CCTV would prove it, but he still said that I was two drops short on my last shift and I know that's a lie." He was in full swing now.

"Where is the recording?"

"Oh that'll be in the office, only that's locked."

The officer raised his hand as he said "That's OK. Now will you do something for me?"

"What?"

"I'll ring you in the morning before you go off, and you give me a list of the drops you've made. Will you do that?"

"Sure. Thank you." He breathed a sigh of relief as though a weight was about to be lifted.

"I like your idea of showing the camera, keep on doing that will you?"

"Course I will."

It had crossed the policeman's mind that maybe the footage wasn't being recorded if the boss was on the fiddle, also previous ones could have been destroyed so there was a chance this one could be seized before anything could be done about it. He returned to the station and requested to leave early as he wanted to follow up the job in the morning but it was suggested that CID would handle it which annoyed him as he had done the initial work and still had loose ends to tie. After much discussion with his seniors, plus the fact CID staff were rather involved with a more serious problem, he was allowed to carry on but with another PC as back up.

As arranged, he rang the cashier and took a note of the canister numbers. He had been allocated a rookie to accompany him, and at 10am they arrived at the station asking to see the manager. He took his time coming out of the office not looking very pleased to see them.

"Yes, can I help you?" he asked.

The older man said in a quiet voice "Maybe we could talk in your office sir?"

Reluctantly he led them into the rather pokey windowless little room where shift sheets, vouchers and empty canisters were strew across the desk.

"Oh I see you are cashing up sir?"

"Yes, and I am in rather a hurry so if you could tell me what it is you've come for....."

"Well it's about the money you see. Is it all in order today would you say?" The officer picked up the sheets before the man could stop him. "Oh that's interesting."

"What is?" The manager now looked most uncomfortable especially as the young PC was removing the CCTV footage from the machine. Fleece was feeding the police with all they needed, directing them to look at the list of drops. The officer pulled a scrap of paper out of his pocket and handed the sheet to his assistant.

"Just read me the numbers in that column would you?"

The young man slowly read the numbers as his elder checked them on his own list then said "Oh that's strange."

"What is?" the manager jumped in.

The first officer took the sheet where he knew two night drops had been crossed through and a shortage had been recorded.

"Could you explain that to us please sir?"

The man was trembling but shrugged and said "Well we seem to have a thief, been suspecting it for some time."

"But I notice those two canister are on your desk. How do you explain that?"

"They.....they were empty of course. It's obvious isn't it?"

"Oh I think it's very obvious sir. Now, would you mind emptying your pockets?"

"I certainly would. You have no right."

Ignoring him the older man said "Go ahead lad, remember what I told you."

His assistant took a pair of gloves from his pocket and started the search much to the objection of the manager.

"Well, what have we here?"

Along with loose change were two rolls of notes which looked as though they hadn't been undone.

"Now if we count those, how much do you think we will find?"

The man was now lost for words but Fleece hadn't finished yet, putting thoughts into the officers mind.

The young policeman asked "What is it?"

"Can't you smell it?"

The manager had had enough and was beginning to feel he was being set up. "What smell, there's no smell here."

"On the contrary there is a definite smell, one that I detest. It's of liars and thieves, and people who blame someone else for their crimes."

"You've got nothing on me. Prove it."

There was a deathly pause as the young man placed himself directly behind the manager and the older officer sniffed the rolls of notes, then the piles of notes which were banded ready for collection.

Very slowly he said "You see sir, I have what's known as a nose. That means I sniff out things. Years of experience I expect, but I know when someone is lying. Now you have a very distinct smell about you, it's on your clothes, on your breath and on things that have been in your pocket, even for a short while, whereas those that you have only touched for a moment only bear the slightest suggestion that you've been in contact with them."

The man had gone pale but still felt he could argue his way out. "Rubbish. You still can't prove anything."

"Right, we must have this lot sent to the lab for examination. Get the evidence bag."

"No you can't, this money has to go away today."

It was the rookie's turn to speak. "Or the oil company will be down on you like a ton of bricks. Now how will you explain that?"

Knowing he had done his job Fleece left the police to deal with the case but called the young spirit guide to let him know his friend would be alright from now on. Quite an easy task really, and as long as those in body heeded their instincts, justice would always be done.

Chapter 4

Mildew was exchanging thoughts with Tisun before the latter left to plant the fake handprints.

"I'm curious as to who the new leader of the Ladydogs could be."

"What makes you think it is someone new?"

"Oh something I heard in passing from the others. Seems she doesn't come out on calls, just leaves the rest to do the actual work while she oversees everything."

Tisun wasn't really in the mood to bother who she was at the moment, but with the female pack involved at the school, he couldn't afford to let any fragment go unnoticed. He had learned in the past that the tiniest snippet had often been the key to the success of an entire operation.

"Wonder why they chose a new one. The old one seemed to be ousted suddenly but for no apparent reason."

Mildew felt he knew more than his boss now. "Well, I understood that this new one had come in and simply taken over."

"Oh, I can see that happening in our pack!" Tisun knew there had to be more to this. No leader would allow that unless...... "She must have a hold over one or maybe all of them, or even the previous one."

This was a little hiccup the males could do without at this crucial time, and although it may not affect them, Tisun didn't like anything going on that he couldn't monitor.

"Well get chatting to the ones at the school. Try and find out as much as you can. I'm sure you can charm the information out of at least one of them."

Mildew recognised the sarcasm in the command but knew it had to be done.

Tisun left to undertake the unknown plan ahead of him but his mind went back for a moment to the one love of his entire existence. Pippa had been special, having spent much spiritual time together as well as earth lives, they were almost as one and when working together, each could sense what the other would do. Whatever had happened, Tisun would never be drawn on it, he even tried to wipe her out of his existence as even the slightest memory was extremely painful. But it had left a complete distrust of females for it had been one particular bitch that had caused the trauma that had separated the two lovers for ever.

He gave himself time to compose himself and be in complete control of his actions. His spiritual senses must be on full concentration until this was finished, and he could not relax for a single moment.

First, he did a quick sweep of the warehouse, taking a mental copy of the concave footprints, then over the school where he duplicated the image of the convex hand ones. No one could have seen him make the placements for it happened in a millisecond. He had previously selected ten venues and now there was an image lying as if misplaced at each, but inside every one was a small section of his spirit, all separate but mentally connected. The danger lay in the fact that if one was destroyed, it would tear part of him away, so the skill would be to withdraw any one at a crucial moment thus leaving his entire being in tact. This was why he had to undertake this dangerous act alone as messages couldn't be passed from one soul to another, however fast.

He waited, the tension heightening his exceptional powers until they were almost giving off electrical waves and humming like a pylon, but he knew how to keep these sensations under control. As if someone had triggered a beam he knew that one of the fake handprints had been observed for there was a presence over it. It could have been amusing if it hadn't been so deadly for there seemed to be a group of beings hovering and arguing as to why the print was there. But what were they going to do about it? It didn't take long for him to realise the answer, they were going to destroy it.

He pulled that part of him out just in time, but annoyed that they hadn't collected it and taken it back to some place he could trace, as quickly as they had arrived, they had gone. He concentrated on the other placings but there seemed to be no interest in them.

"Not very efficient." he thought. Surely if they had found one they would check to see if any other stray prints had been dropped anywhere, but they didn't seem to be bothered, or were they? Tisun always judged others like himself, but just because he was thorough, didn't mean that they would be also. But couldn't that be a trap? In this game nothing could be taken for granted.

He drew back to look at the picture as a whole. The print that had been destroyed was nearest to the school. On reflection it didn't seem that the Ladydogs had paid any attention to the handprints, although they knew they were there and it had been assumed that they didn't know what they were, so had dismissed them. There was also the possibility that all the prints were not being placed by the same group or force, but by individual cells, so there may be no connection between them, whatever shape they were.

Quickly he contacted Mildew to monitor any of the Ladydogs pack that he could find, and ordered King to go and help him. After a moment's consideration, he removed the remaining fake prints from their positions and joined the others at the school.

"Any interest been shown in the existing handprints?" he asked them.

"Not that we've noticed, but I've found out the name of the new leader." Mildew seemed pleased. "It's Raine."

"Doesn't sound familiar, but good work anyway."

Quickly Tisun did a reconnoitre of the premises but everything appeared the same.

"Wait!" he shouted to the others. "Everything is the same, but why?"

"They have stopped." Mildew yelled, "No more have been placed. There's the same amount now as there was before."

"So what's caused it?" King asked.

Tisun was silent for there could only be one possible answer.

Mildew was still gnawing at the fact that the pack had been brought to the school by Dinky under the pretence of there being a bullying problem. It seemed strange that some prints, regardless of which kind, had been placed there, plus the fact that the Ladydogs were possibly involved in some way.

Tisun let him ponder for a while then asked "Come up with the answer yet?"

"Not exactly, as there are bits of the puzzle we haven't found yet. But we weren't brought by chance, there has to be a reason."

"I was aware of that."

Mildew was now trying to get him to describe what had gone on when the print was found, still believing that his leader had been observing from afar but he was left still wondering.

Clemence was standing in front of the class containing Hannah, and the other three pack members, Redhead, the quiet girl and Dinky. The teacher was determined to get even for being made to look so silly in front of the head and was going to pick on Hannah at every opportunity, but the other three were ready for her. With them all being in one place, Tisun ordered Mildew to watch them while he and King examined the handprints at close range. After a few moments they went to the warehouse to check the ones there but to their surprise an obvious change had taken place for the footprints had fused into one solid mass encasing the warehouse, but the perimeter ones had gone completely.

"What do you make of that?" Tisun stated rather than asking a question.

King's nose was working overtime, covering every inch of the place.

"Well?" Tisun was eager to know.

"The worst it could be." King was solemn.

There was an awful silence as the truth sank in for King had detected a substance known to them simply as 'Ultimate'. What had been deposited in this place was the most deadly threat to the spirit world imaginable for it ripped souls away from their area, plunging them into a turmoil of eternal wandering, never having a base or home from which to work. There would be no chance of ever contacting their loved ones or helping those in body in times of need, and there would be no helpers or guardians to look after souls on earth or totally in spirit. It could result in a world where no good existed in any form. A similarity can be made to the planets that get knocked off their orbit and leave their own solar system to travel for ever on a fruitless journey, belonging nowhere or to anyone. But in this case the souls would be in eternal torment.

The question was not why it had been placed, for the evil source need have no specific reason apart from removing the good forces from its area, but more why should it be put here in particular and if possible the pack needed to establish by whom.

The dogs returned to base and called the group together so that they could inform them of the danger on their doorstep. Although unseen by the earthly beings, these people going about their everyday business were possibly in the front line of attack and could be separated from their souls in an instant.

It was now essential to check on the convex handprints to see if they were acting in the same way, or could it be they were the opposite and could be forming a guard. Tisun and Mildew voiced their concerns about the school and the Ladydogs connection, feeling that they were both playing a part in the bigger picture. Unless a very serious job came in, it was now decided that the pack should be on full alert to move straight away if required, but do any nosing around they thought necessary in the meantime.

It was break time and the girls poured out of the classroom. The two bullies had been told to keep up the pestering of Hannah by doing whatever they considered necessary, but not to get caught. The quiet girl was last as usual, taking in every movement made by the teacher. She had been suspicious for some time about this woman who didn't seem to quite add up. Her outward appearance bore no resemblance to her spiritual side and it seemed almost as if she were being played like a puppet with no will of her own. Redhead was pacing the bullies who were by now very uncomfortable whenever she was near. Dinky was free to roam and was hovering outside the school building. She brushed against one of the handprints and it moved away from her. Curiosity made her move towards it, and it moved away again, stopping at a set distance from her. She rose and placed herself above it, but as she descended onto it, the print took off again, but still within the same distance.

"Oh we want to play games do we?" she mocked but suddenly wished she hadn't. It started to vibrate and glow and increase in size until it was taller than she was and as she tried to move, it enveloped her completely, the fingers not squeezing, but emitting a warm comforting feeling that made her relax into it. As quickly as it started, it released her and resumed its size and position.

She trembled for a few moments, then looking round the rest of the prints to check they were unchanged, hurried back to the others.

This little episode had been observed by the male pack with great interest. It could be possible that the convexes were from a good source placed as protection, but Tisun wondered why the one that had been found had to be destroyed. He imagined that it could be to stop it getting into the wrong hands, or that they suspected an evil source had duplicated it and so would take that action. He thought that maybe he should have left the others in place longer to see what happened but he felt that a game of wits was going on until each side knew what they were fighting.

Another important fact was being debated. Originally all the handprints were inside the school, but the one that had taken Dinky into its grasp along with a few others were hovering outside, yet the total number had not increased, almost as though a selected amount had been delegated and although appeared motionless, could travel at will if the need arose.

The Beagles were returning from a call when they sensed a very strong feeling of grief in their vicinity. Without even a nod they both detoured until they homed in on the source. There in the lounge sat an elderly lady clutching a photo of a Pekinese and talking to it as if her world had come to a sudden end.

"Oh Pixie, why don't you let me know you are with me?" she sobbed.

Cello noticed the dog hovering near them.

"Is that you?" he asked.

The dog confirmed it and sidled up to the two friends.

"I often come, but it upsets me to see her so sad. So I go away again."

"Well, that's easily sorted." Noodle said casually.

"It is? How?" Pixie was getting quite excited now.

"Well just a minute. Tell me, have you been able to get through yet?"

The little tail was waving over her back now. "Oh yes, I meet her in her sleep, but when she wakes, she doesn't remember, and I try really hard to make her know I'm here. But it doesn't work."

With a nod from his mate, Noodle soothed the lady into sleep and they gradually entered her dream world. The change was amazing. She and Pixie were together, there were no tears and they were walking along a path lined with trees and the hint of sunlight making patterns as they walked. The Beagles met them and they all conversed in thought as though it was the usual thing to do. After a moment Cello started to communicate with the lady, not in a light hearted way, but going deep into her subconscious. He told her that in her waking time she was blocking these wonderful sensations with her earthly grief and while she continued in this way, Pixie was finding it difficult to get through, which in turn was upsetting her.

"What do I do?" she wondered.

"Open your mind and your inner self. Listen, be aware because that way you will notice more and feel when she is visiting. She has little tasks to do so think of her as being at work and when she has finished she will come home. It is difficult to understand this from the earthly level, but some day you will understand. For now, enjoy her in her spirit form and then she too will be content."

To make sure this information was fresh in her mind, the dogs woke her, letting the recent pictures become implanted in her memory. She could even feel the weight of Pixie as she lay across her feet.

"You should be alright now," Cello said as they were about to leave.

"You can always call us, if she needs a nudge now and then. We'll hear you." Noodle added, and they were gone.

Tisun was hovering between the warehouse and the school when he was aware of a strong presence with him.

"Come." was all he heard but recognised the commanding tone as Ellis, a member of the Danes.

No one knew how many were in this select pack, who the leader was or if in fact they had one. All that was known was that it seemed to consist entirely of Great Danes with extremely high intellect. Their work was never broadcast, and only they were aware of how many times their services were required to rid the earth and surrounding space of the evil that often threatened. So if they were summoning Tisun, it had to be important. He couldn't imagine that they would need his help so his mind raced as he followed the dog to a safe distance.

There were no niceties with this group and Ellis came straight to the point.

"Will you get out of the warehouse area. Now." It wasn't a request, it was definitely an order.

"We aren't in it, and I'm sure you know the reason why." Tisun wasn't one to be put down easily.

"You will ruin everything we've planned if you don't withdraw your attention. Leave it completely alone."

"So why not go ahead and get it over with?" Tisun knew the answer but was trying to find out a bit more.

"You are not that stupid. You know that to go in to soon would only result in the place being reactivated."

"And to leave it too late would mean the evil has got its hold and will carry out its attack or penetration, or whatever it has planned."

"It has to be a precise moment and we don't need any interference. It could prove fatal."

Tisun let the thought sink in then said. "I know the sense of it, but can you tell me one thing?"

"I doubt it."

"The handprint marks at the school, are they related?"

"Of no interest." was all that was replied.

"What about the Ladydog Pack?"

"Of no interest."

"So you are saying you just want the warehouse clear, but the rest is ours?"

"I imagine it's about your level."

Tisun felt his back coming up but said nothing.

"One last thing." Ellis ordered. "No messages, no transmitted thoughts. Understand? You deal with your pack in your own way but no communication regarding this until the place has been neutralised."

"You have my word."

Whether his words were acknowledged or not Tisun could only imagine for Ellis had departed as though he had never been, leaving no trail that could be followed.

As he headed back Tisun was deciding how best to make the pack loose interest in the warehouse and an old trick was to give the dogs something tastier to get their teeth into, so he would concentrate on the power of the handprints and try and make that more important for the time being.

Cello and Noodle seemed to be on the go more than ever and had been called to a small caterer who was supplying sandwiches to local shops. One in particular noticed that the food didn't look fresh but when he had confronted the trader had been told it was all perfectly to standard and was checked regularly, which didn't exactly convince the customer. Noodle's nose soon told him the complaint was right so made his way to the sandwich man's premises for a good sniff around there. What he found was horrifying. The place was dirty with bits of food lying on the floor. There was no sign of any gloves or protective clothing and next to a sack of rolls was a packet of cleaning fluid. Cello joined him to say that the man had taken some out of date packets of food to the back of his van and had relabelled them to appear in date, then sold them to another customer. The whole setup was not only illegal but was food poisoning waiting to happen. Something must be done and quickly.

The dogs had various ways of attracting the attention of humans but sometimes the simplest ones worked very well. Noodle set about locating a health inspector who was driving near to one of the shops that sold the sandwiches. Using his skill he made the person's mouth go very dry, and when the man reached for his bottle of water, he couldn't find it for Noodle had made it roll under the seat out of sight. By now one of the shops was in sight and the desire for a drink was so great, the inspector stopped and went into the shop to buy a bottle of water. As he reached into the chiller, Noodle knocked down a pack of sandwiches onto the floor at his feet. As the man bent down to pick it up, he immediately knew that it wasn't fresh and took it to the counter. After explaining who he was, the shopkeeper said he hadn't been happy with the supplier and was looking for another and willingly showed him an invoice which came with the goods each day.

"I see there is a name and a mobile number but no address." The inspector pointed out. "Do you know where he trades from?"

The shopkeeper looked again at the invoice. "I never noticed that. No I've no idea."

The inspector decided to visit other small shops in the area and got back into his car.

"That's strange," he thought as he noticed that his missing bottle of water was now on the seat beside him alongside a scrap of paper with an address on it. Without hesitation, he drove to the place which appeared to be locked. A dog's bark attracted his attention and he could see what looked like a cross breed barking at him from the side entrance. As he cautiously looked down the alley, the dog ran along it and barked at a side door.

"What is it little feller? Been locked out or are you hungry?" The man laughed. The dog seemed friendly and was wagging its tail as if it knew where it was so the man joined him but as he got to the door, the dog jumped up at a window quite agitated.

"Ok feller, let's have a look." The inspector was a little wary as you never knew what you might find when you peered through windows and he'd had a few shocks before. But the sight that met him filled him with disgust for he was looking at the back room where the food was packaged ready for delivery. There was nobody working so it appeared to be a one man business.

"Well thank you......." he looked down to where the dog had been but it had obviously run off. Strange that it seemed to be telling him where to look then disappeared. He felt for the piece of paper in his pocket, but that too had gone. However it wouldn't take long for his department to deal with this disgusting way of robbing people as well as putting them at risk.

Cello and Noodle were satisfied with the speedy conclusion but agreed that they both preferred their own image as opposed to the one Cello had adopted to suit the purpose.

"Bet you had ticks." Noodle joked "and you'd better not give them to me."

"Very funny." was the reply as they returned to base.

With the warehouse situation having been taken out of their hands, Tisun was still curious as to the random handprints dotted about the school, not so much their movements, but who had placed them and their purpose. It still seemed to be a strange coincidence that they appeared just after the warehouse bunch, unless.....

"Of course," he jumped, "they've been copied but altered."

"Why?" the others wanted to know.

"Oh not for any evil purpose, something could be trying to scare the earthlings, or they could be a bunch of do-gooders who don't know what they're meddling with."

"But the earthlings can't see them, can they?"

Tisun thought for a moment. "Not as far as we know, but there are always the ones who can see into the spiritual, and we're still not sure where the Clemence character fits into all this.

Mildew raised the point "But the Ladydogs can see them, that's for sure."

"And why haven't they taken any notice of them? I would if they appeared near me." Blue said then after a moment "Also, something was quick enough to scoop up that dummy you left to draw them out."

"Agreed," Tisun realised something now, "but they didn't bother with the others did they, so either they weren't important or they didn't trace them, just the one near the school."

"So they are only concentrating in that one area." was the unanimous response.

There was a moment while all reflected upon the comments, then Tisun raised himself up to his full height.

"They have to be behind it." he faced the pack, "The Ladydogs are playing some sort of game and it's got something to do with why we were dragged into the mix."

"I've been wondering that from the start," Mildew snorted, "that Dinky's a bit too friendly for my liking."

"Oh there's more to it than that." Tisun was serious now. "I think they are into something that's got too big for them to handle alone and that's why we were called."

"So now do we tell them to get on with it?" King asked not seriously expecting any sort of agreement.

"You bet we don't, but it may not be a bad idea to let them think we've lost a bit of interest." Tisun confirmed.

"Oh God, that means they'll send the nympho to pull me in again." Mildew tried to look harassed but the others weren't fooled for a second.

"All go about your other tasks for now, there's something I want to check out." It was obvious Tisun had switched off and the conversation was at an end, but there were various comments as he left suggesting he had all the best jobs.

Blue had been spending some time at Heathrow helping the drug sniffing dogs. He liked to keep his hand in and could often save his friends quite a bit of time by using his unseen nose to help root out packages whether being carried externally or internally and he was never wrong, It had been quite a busy session and he thought he had better return to base for a while as he was anxious to keep up with the school matters.

His senses pulled him to a house on the outskirts of a city. There seemed to be a weary call for help coming from a very lovable source and his curiosity drew him to home in on it. He found a frail elderly lady sitting in her chair in the living room at the back of the house chatting away. Her guardian was in presence and at first Blue thought the two were having a spiritual conversation, but then realised it wasn't the case, so he moved to the chair, settled just above the floor and placed his head on the lady's lap.

"And about time too, where have you been?" Her hand reached out and stroked his fur. "It's about time you had a hair cut?"

Blue would have loved to have expressed the mirth but when she continued he felt the sadness of the situation.

"And you haven't had a shave," she was tickling his chin now "what have I told you about coming to visit me without having a shave?"

He knew she could feel him but obviously not see him, so he tried another tactic. The words he would have spoken in body he thought into her soul.

"You know I am here."

"Of course I know, don't I always, only you don't come so much now and I get lonely."

Blue now spoke to the guardian asking the lady's name and was she speaking to her late husband, and had he been visiting her. His reply confirmed his thoughts. The lady is called Beatrice and her husband, Ben used to come regularly but had moved on so his visits were not so frequent.

"But she knows I'm here, but doesn't see me?" he questioned.

"She can't hear you either, but she is very aware of any presence and we converse in our own way. Watch."

"Beatrice."

"Just a minute I'm talking to Ben. He hasn't had a shave you know."

"But there is someone else here this time, it isn't Ben. It's a friend."

The hand went out to Blue's head again. "Who are you then?" she asked aloud.

The guardian nodded to indicate he should communicate.

"My name is Blue, I am a dog."

"A Dog!"

"They have dogs in spirit you know. I work."

Again her hand went out and stroked his head. "What kind are you?"

"I'm a cocker spaniel."

"You're too big for one of those."

Blue sank to floor level. "How about that, this is my real size."

She bent and stroked him for a while. "I had a dog once, felt a lot like you." After a moment she sat up. "Why are you here?"

"I thought I heard you calling for help, and I came, that's what we do."

"Whose we?" she was beginning to feel a bit suspicious now.

"The other dogs I work with, we do all sorts of things. We help people."

The guardian said "She has been asking for help, but I can only comfort her, I can't solve her problems."

Blue acknowledged this information with the reply "Maybe I can." He drew close to Beatrice and mentally homed into her inner self.

"What troubles you?"

"I don't want to go. I like it here." She looked very sad now.

"Where don't you want to go?"

The tears were starting to run. "They say it's only for a week while they go on holiday, but I'm happy here and I talk to angel" she pointed over her shoulder referring to her guardian, "so why can't I stay here?"

"Can you look after yourself?"

"Not much. But meals come, and someone comes in to help me get washed and dressed."

The guardian pulled Blue to one side and conversed in a way Beatrice wouldn't hear.

"They have told her it's only a week but it will be permanent. They say she has dementia and is always talking to people in her imagination but those in body don't understand that she is very spiritually aware. I think she has picked up on whispers and worked out she has to leave here for good and that's what's upsetting her."

"Can she manage?"

"Physically not really, she needs help and the family say they can't take her in so there's no other possibility."

Blue was deep in thought for a moment then many messages flew back and forth between the pack. He checked that the guardian would be with her wherever she went then snuggled up to her.

"Beatrice."

"Yes."

"Would you mind where you were living as long as someone you loved very much was there with you?"

"Of course I wouldn't but that's not possible. I love my family but they are too busy to bother about me and all the others have gone."

"Well supposing I told you that if you were to go to this home where you could be cared for, there would be somebody you love waiting there for you. What would you say?"

"You're telling me lies. Don't be unkind."

"Beatrice. Your husband and your dog will be waiting there for you."

"How can they be?" she was crying now "they died, they died."

"Only from their bodies. They still exist in our world, my friends have contacted them, and if you wish it, they want to be there with you for as long as you are on earth."

The dog pack had been very busy, and both Ben and their dog, although they had tasks of their own agreed that to stay in presence for the rest of Beatrice's life would make her earthly days pleasurable. It didn't matter if people thought she was crazy, away with the fairies or whatever expression they cared to choose, she would be happy with those who loved her until it was her time to pass on and join them in their existence. It was also noted that the time wasn't that far off so the powers above agreed to the arrangement for the sake of the lady's happiness.

Now she was stroking Blue's head but the tears that fell were tears of relief.

"You really mean it?"

"I really mean it. Ask Angel. She's coming with you too. Be quite a gathering it seems."

"Then I can't wait. I am so happy. What was your name?"

"I'm called Blue."

"Then I love you Mr Blue. Will you come and see me as well?"

"You just try and stop me."

She felt the tongue lick her cheek and held her hand to the spot which felt moist. Her angel took over as Blue left knowing he had helped Beatrice in her later years, but he wondered how many more were in her position, spending their days in loneliness because they were not aware of the spiritual support which was there waiting for them to tune in.

There was a lot going on at the school in different ways. For a start the dog pack realised the handprints were changing. The fingers were shortening to such an extent that they looked almost like circles and the palm was taking on a shape of its own and it was happening simultaneously as though a message had be sent to each one to alter and move as one. But that was not all. As they watched each image split into two identical ones then again so that each was positioned in a set of four.

The dogs now knew what was happening but Tisun voiced it for everyone.

"Paw prints, of course, that's why they've now formed this pattern, but look, they are grouped differently, go and check out their exact locations."

Within seconds the lads were back.

"I've counted nine outside near the wall." said Cello.

"And I've seen nine inside the school but centred mainly still round the staff room," added Noodle.

They turned to King waiting for his reply.

"One, a bigger one positioned higher than the rest, probably overseeing whatever their plan is."

Tisun was trying to make sense of the tactics. "Nine, nine, and one. One nine, nine. Nine one nine. Total nineteen. It doesn't make a lot of sense as an attack plan and doesn't cover enough ground for an observation set up, so what is going on?"

"Well they didn't hurt Dinky, in fact they seemed to be protecting her so they can't be evil can they?" Mildew was also summing up.

Another thought hit Tisun. "That's why the other images weren't destroyed."

The pack wondered what he was thinking so he explained.

"If whatever force it is, is concentrating its efforts solely on the school, the other images wouldn't be any interest to them, but if I had been in that position, my curiosity would have made me wonder why they were randomly placed."

"Unless they didn't know they were there." Mildew thought.

"Of course they must have known, even the simplest spirit energy would have picked up on them. No, they ignored them, and I bet that was a test to see what we would do."

King had been listening carefully "But surely the most important fact now is to find out who they are."

"Probably easier said than done," Mildew didn't think it was that simple. "I feel they are playing us, but not as a game, I think there's more to it."

"Spot on," Tisun said "we must be more on the alert than ever until we know, but I don't think we can force their hand. However, if they think we have lost interest they may just up the action."

Nobody argued this point as they all knew their leader didn't think or act without a lot of contemplation, but all guessed he knew more than he was telling them.

But the males were not the only ones watching the paw prints, the Ladydogs too were wondering what was going on at the school and it didn't help there current frame of mind for they were very restless.

School had finished for the day and they were in a huddle near the cloakroom.

"But why do we have to stay here all the time?" Redhead was very impatient and liked loads of action. This ticking over routine was winding her up like a spring and she was ready to explode.

"Better do as Madam says" Dinky warned her "you know what happened last time when you scared the bullies. She threatened you what would happen the next time you were stupid."

"What can she do?" Hannah cut in. "It's all right for the rest of you but I'm pretty pig sick of this act she's got me playing. I'm not meek and mild, I don't get bullied, I fight my own battles, and I can tell you I've had it up to here."

"Because," the quiet girl spoke now, "you know the hold she has. If we don't tow the line, we will all be sent off the way our leader was."

They were all quiet now. It had happened in the blink of an eye, one minute they were the happy little band working under Ruby, a friend they had known in many earth lives and for whom they had the greatest respect. She had tremendous compassion and her soul purpose was similar to the dog pack, to help those in crisis, to calm and comfort and leave a trail of peace in her wake. So when Raine had arrived saying their beloved friend had been despatched, their first reaction of surprise turned to anger. They wanted answers but all they were told was that if they didn't comply they would follow the same fate, never to return to this area ever again. When Redhead had demanded to know more, Raine had turned on her and paralysed her entire spirit, something none of them had ever experienced. She had been held in that state for some time until Raine decided to release her. This power had frightened the rest into submission and therefore dare not cross her.

But emotions, especially spiritual ones can run high, and when a person is reaching breaking point, they somehow find the courage and power to fight back and the female pack were starting to enter this zone.

Having learned of this situation, Tisun was certain that this was the bitch that had banished his beloved Pippa, for there weren't many who could undertake this kind of horrendous task so easily, and then get such sadistic pleasure from the outcome. He always felt that it had to be a coward that could only get rid of the opposition in order to rule. A true power had no need of such actions. So what threats were Pippa and Ruby that they had to suffer such a horrible existence?

Chapter 5

An urgent call had come in to the dog pack concerning an increase of explosives being shipped into the country and King was about to leave with Blue when another message was received saying there seemed to be a large concentration of houses which were being rented but the people were only there during the day at odd times, and never communicated with their neighbours.

"First, you'd better check out the vehicles arriving and send word if you need help" Tisun advised King who didn't hang around for any further instructions and knew the drill if he needed assistance.

"Same for me?" Blue asked.

"For now, but see what you can find out from the local patrol." By this Tisun was referring to the alert dogs in the surrounding area for they were quick to notice the slightest thing.

"Wonder what will be next," Fleece stated, "the requests always come at once don't they?"

"And then you get the long drawn out ones, like the school." Mildew was taking a moment away from the scene to reflect and try to piece all the bits together.

"Can we go and have a nose around?" Noodle looked towards Cello as he asked.

"Better ask boss man." Mildew indicated Tisun.

"We don't want too many hanging around at the moment, we're trying to work out what the objective is." The leader's reply was very concise and they all knew better than to question it. "Anyway, one of the others may call for back up depending on the size of each operation." he added.

This seemed to satisfy them for the moment, but they were always eager to get their teeth into something tasty, sometimes literally!

King was working the port at Dover with some of his old friends. The handlers wondered why the dogs had become so excited, little knowing the brief reunion that was taking place under their noses.

Quickly, the dogs told him that, at a certain time each day, and always on vehicles operated by the same carrier, they were picking up a distinct explosive scent and feared that a terrorist cell was being supplied up north as that was where some of the suspect loads were being taken.

"So how much has been found?" King needed to know.

There was a silence as the pals exchanged looks. "We haven't found any substance?"

"But that's impossible, we can sniff out anything."

"Ok, come with us on the next one, its due in about an hour and you'll see."

King was baffled, these were sniffers of the highest calibre and if anything was there, they would find it, and always had done in the past, so what was going wrong now? On the promise he would be back shortly, he returned to base to report to Tisun, who, after a moment's pondering looked King straight in the eye.

"There is one possibility. Only seen it a couple of times but it has the border control left scratching their heads."

"What?"

"Now listen carefully because you won't take it in to start with."

The two dogs sat alone in conference while the leader explained the strangest operation to his mate. There was silence while King tried to grasp the situation but now he was being warned not to divulge this to anyone but use it to apprehend the traffickers. He must not even tell the working dogs at the port what he was doing, but just depart afterwards leaving them wondering. He hoped he could carry it out and knew he would be entirely alone when the time came.

Blue had homed in on one of the locations, and as soon as he approached he knew what was going on here. All the curtains were drawn at this house and he looked for a tell tale cable which was tapping electricity from another address. Quickly he found one of the spiritual patrol dogs who soon showed him many such dwellings. One or two were a bit off the beaten track but some were semi detached in the suburbs and any observer would have thought it a bit stupid to place them where they could easily be identified.

The guide now took Blue to where the tenants were on the premises, and sure enough they were tending rooms full of plants being kept at a certain temperature.

"A few pounds worth here, or will be when it's marketed." Blue commented.

"Especially when you multiply it by all the other 'greenhouses'," the dog used the word they had adopted for premises growing cannabis plants, "they won't be too happy when we blow this one."

"So do you reckon they are all being run by the same group?" Blue was taking a mental note of the description of the two men and one woman.

"We know so. Some of us have been checking them out, there's another two as well as these and they do the rounds continually."

"Where do they actually live?"

"Oh, not in any of these of course. Tracked them to the next town."

"Well, "said Blue, "you've certainly made it easy, now to close 'em down eh?"

There was a pause. "Is there a problem with that?"

"Well," the guide was hesitant "you see we aren't the only spirits around here, in fact can we move away now please?"

"Sure." Blue followed him to a distance from the house. "Go on."

"There is a very protective force around all the places these people cultivate their little gardens, and we've had more than one warning not to meddle or else."

"And who has given you these warnings and in what form?" Blue knew that this wasn't just the ordinary little closure and became more interested and added "And that's why you called us."

"Yes, I'm sorry, but they seem to be a rather forceful bunch."

"Well, you need have no more dealings with it, we'll take it from here." Blue said how grateful the pack was for the information and ushered the dog on his way, noticing the mixture of relief but guilt which followed him. It was the only action, as some of these helpful little sentinels were invaluable when it came to observation, but weren't the sort you needed by your side in a crisis.

Back at base the members of the pack were summing up their requirements. King would be acting alone for now due to the secrecy of the operation but Gerald was on standby in case things got nasty. He wouldn't know the details of what was going on but would act on instruction from Tisun. He also had another couple of Rottweiler pals as back up and not many humans or spirits would be brave enough to challenge the trio when they were in full attack form. They were only used in extreme cases but the pack sensed that not only may they be useful at the port but also on the drug operation, for there was a definite evil presence there. This came as no surprise for anything involving power or riches came at a price, with the evil entities trading their assistance but their pawns not realising what they had let themselves in for until it was too late.

It was time for the ferry carrying the target lorries to arrive, the dog handlers little realising they had an extra nose on their side. King watched as the first was directed into the sheds, and following Tisun's advice headed straight for the cab and sniffed the driver.

"So that's it." he thought, no wonder they've been getting away with it.

The duty dogs were checking under the vehicle and going through all the usual places. Other customs officers were using their special equipment checking for clandestines which was always an ongoing problem. Quickly King moved to the other two lorries which were waiting in line and did the same check on the drivers. All positive. Time to get to work with his comrades on the first vehicle.

"What is it boy?" one of the handlers was wondering why his dog was pulling him to the cab. The driver, who was being questioned while the cab was undergoing a search, seemed quite relaxed and showed no signs of stress, in fact appeared eager to help. The dog was frantically pawing at the back of the seat, and it was only when officers moved the driver away he began to look uneasy.

"But there's nothing here boy. You having us on again?" The handler looked surprised at the dog's persistence, as he wouldn't be dragged away but kept pulling towards the back of the seat. If it had been left to the dog's instinct he would have given up a long time ago but King was pushing him to keep up the act.

The word went to other officers to check the cabs of the following two vehicles. King went through the same process with the dogs there, for they had lost the scent but he was pushing them to be diligent, and fortunately they trusted him.

Immediately the first drivers' seat had been taken apart, everything was on full alert and vehicles apart from the three in question were diverted to other examination sheds and full security brought in. The drivers were under arrest and had been taken away for further questioning and although the dogs were allowed a full run, the only places they were interested in were the three drivers' seats, not the passenger ones. The handlers praised the dogs for finding the haul of explosives in the specially designed area of the seats and believed they had stopped this operation in its infancy, whereas it was only due to their diligence that the result had been achieved. The next task was to draw attention to the delivery point, but that was where they would bring in the backup as that could get a bit nasty.

Before he left, the dogs asked King how he had known where to look as the scent had disappeared at some point. He just gave them a knowing look which said "Don't ask" and left to get on with part two, the depository in the north of England.

Briefly he returned to the pack and confirmed to Tisun that it was as he expected but he would certainly remember it for future occasions.

The sniffer dogs had certainly detected explosives, so why did the scent run cold and nothing was found until now? The answer was a trick used by mentalists and illusionists and possibly hypnotists. You see what they want you to see. All the drivers were of this calibre, so when the dogs went on the trail they could control any of their senses, including smell and switch it off at the given time. Likewise the officers could actually be looking at something suspicious but their brain would be told it wasn't there which is why they had never found the way into the seats before. Tisun could recall people actually looking at the physical item, but not seeing it because they were being told not to. This information was not in general circulation as it could act as a warning and hamper the capture of such people, which this case had certainly proved.

Tisun was in distance conference with Mildew who was examining the paw prints for any changes. Although they seemed to be stationary, he noticed each set of paws was changing position within its group whilst the lone one appeared static. Trying a new tactic, he positioned himself in the centre of the outside group which split away from him for a moment as if examining him, then closed in on all sides covering him with a warm relaxing feeling. It was so enjoyable, that it took all his self will to pull himself out and hover a safe distance away.

"Who are you?" he sent out the thought.

The group trembled and he got the impression they were laughing at him, but in a nice way for there was no malice or ill feeling in the air.

Again he asked "What are you? Won't you tell me?"

Still no reply but he knew they were understanding him so he tried another ploy.

"Come on, we're all dogs here, what's going on?"

They must have realised he wasn't going anywhere until he had some sort of explanation but the reply wasn't quite what he expected.

"You will know when we are ready. You are a good person Mildew."

"You know my name." he stated with some surprise, yet with afterthought, realised any power could have known.

It was obvious the meeting had ended for the paws resumed their previous positions quickly as if they had been given a signal.

Mildew was relaying this to Tisun who was still trying to piece the jigsaw together. He now felt the clues were coming in from various sources and it was up to him to sort it and for that reason he needed to stay at base and concentrate as much as possible for it could be the smallest scrap of information that would be the key.

Blue wanted to get his job finished as soon as possible so that as many growers could be caught as soon as possible as many of the plants looked ready for cutting. He had debated whether to leave it and follow the trail to the end product, but so many complaints were coming in from local residents he thought he had better act now. He had made sure the local police had all the details and much to his delight learned they were planning an immediate raid

After consultation with Tisun, Gerald and his two buddies were sent to liaise with him at a certain house. He took a few moments to

71

calm them down as this lot were so excited to be called in that he was afraid they may 'cock it up' if they got carried away.

"There is usually one who sits in a car just round the corner and alerts them if he sees any police etc. You will watch him," he indicated to one of the pair, "and you in turn tell us."

"I wanted to come in when you broke the door down, I'd have had them, all of them." was the disappointed answer.

"Which is exactly why you have been given the task you have. Now, if you don't like it you can piss off back to where you came from." Blue often surprised helpers by his forcefulness but he stood no nonsense and everyone soon realised it was better not to mess with him.

"Ok, Ok, I was only saying….."

Blue almost snorted, then turned his attention to the others. "Now you," he faced the other helper "I want you out the back in case one of them gets out of a door, window, side entrance, anything. You are responsible for the entire outside of the building. Can you manage that?"

"You bet I can." This dog wasn't going down the path his mate had taken.

"Now Gerald, we have a little bit of work to do before the boys in blue get here," then he looked at the first dog, "we will not be breaking anything down, we work in our way. Is that fully understood?"

"Of course."

Gerald always meant well, but it was calling him to heel that was always the problem.

"Right, positions." Blue ordered. He checked the first dog was ready waiting for the car, then that the second had full knowledge of the exterior before he and Gerald made their way inside.

"Bloody hell, there's enough here to….." he was cut short as Blue sensed the approach of the car, confirmed by the watcher.

"You take that room, I'll take this one." he quickly positioned them upstairs and within a couple of minutes heard the key in the front door. As expected two people went into the downstairs rooms checking on the plants there.

"One's a woman." Gerald thought but Blue silently told him to be still in every way for they didn't know what they were up against and one or both of the people could be very spiritually aware.

After a short time they knew one of them was coming up the stairs and their senses bristled. The woman went to open the door of Gerald's room, then stopped with her hand on the door knob. The dogs froze trying not to disturb the air in the slightest. She turned and went into the bathroom to use the toilet and they almost breathed a sigh of relief, but were back on alert as she returned. The man followed and went into Blue's room at which point both dogs then placed themselves by the door ready to block any exit.

The alert came from the dog guarding the car seconds before the couple received their message that police had appeared from nowhere and were heading for the house.

"Quick get out." the man shouted to the woman.

"I can't, the door's jammed....oh my God!" she screamed

He didn't answer, for he couldn't even get to the door and the words blocked his throat in terror for there in front of him was the most ferocious dog he had ever seen. It had him in its sights and was getting ready to spring.

"Get away," was all he could whisper but the growling covered any sound he could make.

The woman was now wondering if she could get to the window but she knew the moment she moved the terrible dog in front of her would get her. Fright took over and she collapsed, and with a nudge from Gerald, landed right in the middle of the plants, breaking them as she fell. Being Gerald he just couldn't resist standing over her until she came round just to see the terror on her face.

Blue didn't need to do any more than hold his ground until the front door was forced and the place was teeming with police, and as soon as they entered the room he released his hold.

"Get your dog off. Bloody nearly killed me." The man screamed, then realised there was no dog in the room.

The poor woman was just coming round when the officers grabbed her and thinking that it was the dog she fought like mad until she saw there was nothing there. Like the man she started to rant at them to keep their animals under control. The police were all of the same mind, that this pair were so high they were hallucinating.

The third culprit had also been arrested, and he was babbling about a dog that had been in the car although he couldn't understand how it had got in.

"Never mind, sir," one of the officers mocked, "we'll make sure somebody feeds it for you."

"We'll leave the earthly powers to finish their job now, I'm sure you've got plenty to do, but thank you very much, greatly appreciated." Blue had resumed his appearance of the innocent looking cocker spaniel that fooled many, and dismissed the rather disappointed trio.

"I enjoyed it," Gerald said, "but it was over quicker than I'd hoped. I was just getting my teeth into it."

"Speak for yourself, I never got to do anything," the outside dog moaned. "But I did look through the windows, so I had a bit of a laugh."

"Oh I had some fun too. There was quite an unpleasant smell in the car when I left." said the other.

"You didn't?" Gerald tried to sound horrified.

"No, not me, the bloke."

This caused a laugh but Blue had to bring them to order and send them on their way. Not quite all of the comments would be relayed back to base, but sufficient to say the outcome had been successful and could be repeated at other dwellings with the same crew then perhaps they would all have a bite of the bone.

King had located the stash of explosives and was calling for help to draw in the authorities who at this time didn't appear to be paying any attention to the property, but most of the stuff was stored underground so it needed a nudge in the right direction to get them to detect it. The whole surface operation seemed to be a haulage company so any kind of commodity could be moved around the country and abroad. They had the usual checks but everything always seemed perfectly above board, but there again it could be a case of seeing what you were supposed to see if the same technique was being used there as well as at the ports.

The best way to get attention would probably have to be by a roundabout route and King was running this past Tisun.

"I could try and get the local dogs to seem to sniff out the stuff by leading them to it, but it is not on their normal path so it might seem strange for them to suddenly turn up and find something."

"So you're going for the other option?" Tisun knew what was going through his mind.

"Worth a try. Don't see how else we're going to do it."

"How much help do you need?"

King thought. "Got to be the right sort. Might not need too many. Could use the old multi mirror image."

"I'd use our own, don't bring any others in. The Beagles could do it, and Fleece if you need more, but you don't need loads, as long as you get the right effect." Tisun knew it could be done and was happy to leave this dog in charge.

The leader was spending more time contemplating and was getting frustrated as he felt something was staring him in the face, but if so, it was as though a power was blocking it enough so that he didn't notice it. But he wouldn't give up because an inner sense was telling him he would resolve it and he would never rest until he knew the truth.

Dinky had tasted the wine and wanted more. Much as she tried she couldn't get over the wonderful feeling the 'hand' had given her when it embraced her whole being. She wasn't sure which it was but guessed they must all be the same, and now the hands had become paws, she wondered if the effect would be the same. She drifted outside to the wall and hovered in front of the group waiting to see if they responded to her presence. There was nothing. She turned and presented herself, looking over her shoulder to see if this had any effect and sure enough a ripple ran through the group.

"Oh, so you like that do you?" she laughed, but fell silent when there was no other response. "Can you do what you did the other day?" Again all was still. Feeling very disappointed she turned and made her way back to the others.

"What's up with you gloomy pants?" Redhead asked.

"Oh nothing. Just fed up. I want to get back to our proper jobs."

"Don't we all?" Hannah was close to tears. "I hate this body, I hate this job. I'm getting out."

"You can't. She won't let you, how many times do we have to tell you?" Redhead was getting frustrated, not only with the situation but with this girl who didn't seem to be holding it together at all now.

"I don't care. Nothing can be as bad as this." Hannah was sobbing now.

"Yes it can." Redhead reminded her.

"Wait a minute." Dinky cut in. "Hannah, do you trust me?"

"Well, yes, but you're not tied down in a body are you?"

Ignoring the remark she said "Come with me a minute."

"Why?" Hannah didn't move.

"Oh just go with her for God's sake." Redhead almost screamed.

"You should." The quiet girl spoke for the first time.

"Why? What do you know?" Hannah wasn't going to be consoled at any cost, she was too low to listen to any offer of help.

"Come on," Dinky beckoned and the other two physically got hold of Hannah and pushed her to follow. Together the four reached the wall and Dinky called to the paws for help, begging them to look at their friend.

"Well?" Redhead said.

"Shh."

The paws started to move until four sets had encompassed the three physical girls and Dinky. As before, the loving warmth flowed round them and all seemed calm and peaceful. There was no Raine, no rule of terror, only extreme love as a mother would give her precious child.

None of them knew how long they were held there, but slowly were returned to the door leading into the school feeling as though nothing could harm them again. The paws resumed their positions and all was quiet.

Raine had witnessed this little episode and her anger seethed. Whatever this force was it was undoing all her well planned work. She had almost succeeded in bringing Hannah down, Redhead was reacting nicely, and Dinky had been showing signs of strain. The quiet one may not be appearing to take much in but she missed nothing and she was the one who would suffer most watching her pals going through mental torment which was much more effective than any physical one.

But there was much more to this than any of them knew. There had been a special bond between them when they became Ladydogs, something which Ruby knew when she brought them together and had promised to protect them. But no one had reckoned with the evil Raine who would destroy each of them at her pleasure for she knew that they were all sisters, albeit from different litters but with the same mother. In fact they were all Pippa's puppies, and Ruby was their aunt, but they were all unaware of this. When Raine learned that they were about to be told the truth, she had to despatch Ruby and take control herself or she would never be able to fulfil her plan and achieve her ultimate dream.

For now she had thought they were completely in her power, until this other source had appeared which seemed to be working against her. This meant she must up her game, then they would see what she was really made of. But it meant she had to get rid of the paws completely so that nothing could stand in her way, and she must do it first so that it couldn't help the girls. She toyed with the idea that she could easily despatch the stupid pups now which would be less bother, but the thought came to her that if the paws were protecting them, and she did anything to hurt them, the good force would immediately turn on her and then she would still not get her end result. Plus the fact she still didn't know just how powerful this new force was or what it could do. Her pride wouldn't accept it could be her equal, but her sense told her it could be permanently harmful. She decided to let the bullying continue for now for that was keeping the Mildew creature in tow, and if Dinky was still lusting after him, so much the better. Plans can always be changed to suit the situation and there was no way she was going to fail. The prize was too precious.

Tisun had decided to give himself an airing and have a look at one of the operations in the hope it would clear his mind enough to be able to get the answers he was looking for. The drug situation seemed to be under control for now, although it would always be an ongoing problem and Blue would be monitoring it, Mildew was still in situ at the school but that seemed necessary for now until they had more answers, and Fleece was busier than ever as there seemed to be more elderly people being targeted for their life savings. Cello and

Noodle were lined up for the haulage operation under King's direction and Tisun was about to go out and give the premises a once over when he had a contact message from an old buddy. Instantly the two were in conference.

Tankard liked to keep his image of an Irish Wolfhound which seemed to fit his persona. He was such a likeable character who never lost his slow country drawl and laid back attitude but had pulled off some of the most amazing stunts ever known. He and Tisun had worked together on many occasions and were never afraid to call on the other if they felt they could do with a bit of expert help. This dog fooled many into thinking he was well past it, too tired, and couldn't be bothered to get involved which often resulted in the downfall of the opposition. If they had only realised a spirit is never any of these things, and if anything they grow in experience and skill.

"Good to see you my man." Tisun would have shaken hands had he been in body but the greeting held as much respect and affection.

"Well I bin thinking of you and summat tells I that you aint be too 'appy."

Immediately he heard the familiar tones, Tisun felt his spirit lifting and was grateful for his friend's presence.

"Now how did you know?"

"Aah, me nose told I."

"Well there's a lot going on, but what about you. What have you been up to?" Tisun's strength was returning by the moment.

"That aint why I'm 'ere and you knows it."

"You're a canny old fox Tankard. Still like the smell of your pint?"

"Oo aah, I still goes down the local and gets into one of the dogs for a while. There's one who 'as a guzzle in a bowl, so I gets the taste so to speak."

"You'll never change."

"Why should I?" Tankard gave one of his cheeky know-it-all looks which was so reassuring. He made you wonder why you worried about anything at all.

They took a moment to enjoy their reunion but there was obviously more to this than a casual call.

"So, you going to spill, or 'ave I got to drag it out of you?" Tankard took a relaxed position but fixed his eyes on his mate as if he was peering into his very soul.

"Oh there's a lot going on and...." Tisun paused wondering how much this dog already knew, and how deep into his inner self he could probe.

"Best spit it out." Tankard's eyes were unblinking and his comment although casual held the tone of an order.

Slowly Tisun explained everything from Pippa's untimely exit to the current events at the school including the arrival of Raine.

"Aah, wondered when you'd get to 'er."

"You know?" Tisun should have guessed that his friend wouldn't have turned up half cocked, he always did his homework.

This was an eye opener. Up to now, Tisun had been so wrapped up in the grief of losing his beloved soul mate, and although he put on a brave face to the dog pack, he had been missing facts which should have been staring him in the face. Then he would have been aware of Tankard's presence knowing he would have homed in on any danger and was there to help protect him when his defences were not on full alert.

"I've been blind." was all he could utter.

"Aah, we all bin there at some time. You bin there for me, now I be 'ere for you."

A thought hit Tisun like a bullet. Here was the perfect man for the haulage company operation.

"Hey, how about helping on a job?"

"Now yer talking!"

It didn't matter what they did, Tankard knew this would pull his friend out of the depression trough and get him moving and thinking for himself. It may start with a job with no connection to his troubles, but that may not be a bad thing, then if the time was right, he could help sort out the main problem. But this would do for now.

"I'll bring King in, it's his shout you understand."

The acknowledgement came in the form of a simple flick of the tail.

King arrived and was amazed to meet this dog. He had heard many tales from various sources but had never been in his presence.

"This is an honour." he greeted him.

The reply came as a surprise. "You a boozer?"

"Well, I was, when I was in body, and will be again I expect."

"Aah, 'e be a good un. We'll 'ave 'im."

King was so amused by this he almost forgot that he had been summoned for a reason.

"Um, I know we said we'd keep your job in the pack," Tisun hesitated "but my good friend herehas had a lot of experience in this field and he is happy to help us."

"Well why not, as long as the others don't object."

"Speaks 'is mind don't 'e." Tankard laughed.

Tisun quickly said "The Beagles will be in on it too and everyone else has their own task to cope with so no problem."

The three went into conference to discuss the mirror tactic and King raised the point that the three lorries had just been intercepted so tempers could be at a high.

"All the better. Catch 'em with their breeches down." Tankard couldn't wait to get started. "When do we go?"

"May as well get on with it. Tonight when it's dark. There's a security patrol firm that goes round the industrial estate, we'll time it so that they can't miss us, then we'll make sure they call for back up." Tisun was getting his teeth into this now and felt his power returning. "Get the Beagles in so they know what they have to do." he told King

"They done it before?" Tankard asked.

"No. It'll be a first for them."

"Got to learn sometime."

"It's Ok, they're good at taking instruction."

Cello and Noodle arrived and all went into conference. It was decided that while the operation was going on, Mildew would return to base as there seemed to be little action at the school and he could always go back if there were any developments.

As Tankard left, he turned and said to Tisun "Don't forget the mirror."

On his own now, Tisun mused about the last comment. What a strange thing to say. In human form if a group were going on a raid or any kind of job, they would check their equipment carefully, but in the spirit world it didn't work that way. Sometimes inanimate objects may be moved or used, but this wasn't that kind of job. There were no mirrors as such, only the power of thought, illusion and spiritual knowhow. This thought kept racing round his mind as though he was looking at something but not seeing it. The word mirror was everywhere until he had to try and push it away to be able to think about the rest of the plan for that night. Then King came to mind. He had been the first one to mention the word and it didn't take on any significance then, so why now?

As though someone had slapped him in the face it came to him. Tankard had used King to give him a clue to his own problem, but he hadn't picked up on it, so his friend had been forced to come in person to get involved in that particular job, and his farewell comment had been the prod that he needed. The only trouble was he still didn't know the significance and he felt he was being pushed to work it out for himself. Only then would he know the truth.

Most people in Mildew's position would have been bored hanging around waiting for something to happen but he wasn't that sort. On many occasions his patience had paid off in the physical world and in the spiritual. He wasn't likely to trace any mortal bodies at the school, but there could be many things to unearth given time. He had been observing the four Ladydogs and watching the pendulum swing with their emotions and was particularly interested in the paws now for this was definitely a good power but somehow managed to remain cloaked from its identity. It surprised him that no attack had been made on it by Raine or any other evil source and it was left alone to exist at the same place as whatever scheme was going on with the female dogs. The teacher seemed to be a puppet being used for some purpose but there seemed to be no threat from her directly as her vibrations were far too weak. Likewise the bullies, who didn't even know they were part of a plan but just followed their instincts or so they believed.

When he got the call to return to base for the night, he welcomed the break from Dinky's continual advances but felt he was in danger of missing something if Raine took advantage of his absence. Being night time, he couldn't think that she would strike then as the girls were supposed to return to her base for a dressing down. He welcomed the unrest hoping they would take some of it back, but it was a futile hope as he knew Raine would squash them back to nothing if they even tried to object. It seemed the paws would have the place to themselves. But could anything in this game be that simple?

If anyone needed a rest it was Fleece. His heart went out to the frail elderly people who ended up at the mercy of thieves and con artists who were supposed to be the ones who were helping them. In many cases now, he was covering not one, but several cases, some in retirement homes, but many in the folks own homes. Tisun had been good enough to let him have some assistance from helper dogs who watched many places for him allowing him to concentrate on catching the scum. Fortunately the matter was being highlighted in the media, but there were those who found it too easy a picking to let go. As soon as some had been caught another batch reared its ugly head, and soon Fleece found he wasn't getting any sort of break to catch up with the others. As luck would have it, there was another dog group just starting up which was concentrating solely on this menace and so there was a ray of hope that things may ease a little before long.

Raine was furious. Her bitches may not be answering her back directly but they certainly had an air of rebellion about them. They weren't playing her game any longer and she guessed the paws had a lot to do with it. Time for a shake up.

"Right, pay very careful attention." she looked round them individually. "As you all seem incapable of carrying out the simplest task, we are going to change our arrangements." They all stayed motionless which was beginning to annoy her even more. She looked straight at Redhead hoping to goad her into some sort of reaction, but there was nothing. All she got was the fixed stare back at her. She turned her attention to Hannah who also seemed to be in a trance, and Dinky had a daft smug grin on her face as though she was in a far off place.

"And you, you little runt," Raine stormed at the quiet one "aren't worth the space you take, I can't think why you ever joined this group in the first place."

The girls didn't know why they were able to keep up this façade, but it was so easy, almost as if something, or someone was acting on their behalf.

"I've got it." Raine almost screamed "You've being meddling with those paw things. They've made you like this. Well, we'll soon put a stop to that."

"I would think very carefully before attempting any contact with something you don't understand." The voice was slow and soft but held the warning to stay away.

"Who said that?" Raine was spinning round watching each girl carefully. "Which of you is playing tricks?" But this wasn't going to work.

"Oh I see through your little game," she spat "think you can get the better of me do you, well you should have learnt by now, that doesn't work." The last three words were shouted at such a pitch the whole area shuddered from the vibration.

"Right, you like to be static like a load of dummies, well stay like it, especially you," she yelled at Dinky, "then see how your lover boy treats you." She came right up to her as she seethed "He won't even know you exist."

The thought of losing Mildew before she had even hooked him started to get through to Dinky, and Raine was quick to pick up on this weakness but knew she needed to keep the dog's interest at the moment so just retorted "I thought that might hit a nerve."

There was a force strengthening the girls and it was feeding off Raine's anger, so as soon as Dinky started to weaken, a sudden serge was sent to her entire being to give her the will power to hold off against this evil leader. It also put the thought into her mind that the person threatening her was lying.

Although Raine knew she was now fighting a much more powerful being, she had to keep her position at all costs and without warning froze the four where they were. She knew they were still aware of what she was saying and doing, but couldn't respond.

"Let's have this understood. What I say goes. I am the leader of this pack for one reason, that I am greater than any of you, I am more powerful and....."she paused "when I want something, I don't give up until I get it, and if you puny little pups think you can outwit me, you are even more stupid than I thought."

She released them slowly, knowing she had put them all back in their place, but she had made one fatal mistake.

Before Mildew left for the night, he approached the nine paws within the school. Although they floated around as a bunch, they always seemed to return to the staff room, and he wondered if this bore some significance or was it just by chance. He dismissed the latter, for any power of this magnitude didn't do anything without cause. Recalling his pleasant experience with the ones outside, he was keen to see if these reacted in the same way, and he would never refuse a 'spiritual caress' if there was one going.

The staff room was empty and Mildew wondered why he had seen no sign of the paws on his way there and mild panic took hold as he thought they may have left, but that idea was soon answered by a warm feeling close to his side.

"Is that you?" he thought.

"Isn't that why you are here?"

To be answered with another question flawed him for a moment so he tried to turn it around.

"If you know, why ask?"

There was a ripple of mirth as the warmth flowed round him until he was floating in a beautiful place but unable to see who was with him. After a moment he returned to his normal state but knew he was not alone.

"When will you tell me who you are?"

"When the time is right."

He felt he must push it further. "And that will be....?"

"Soon. Be patient Mildew."

Again the personal use of his name gave him a secure feeling so he decided to push further.

"Can I visit the one who sits alone above you?"

The air shuddered. "That is not possible at all, and you must not even consider it."

"And if I tried?"

"You would not succeed."

This left him a bit deflated and feeling rather useless. He liked to be in control but in this situation he was very aware that he wasn't.

Well, he would pass it on to Tisun when he returned to base which was any minute now.

"Hope it cheers him up a bit" he thought to himself.

Was it his imagination, or as he left did he hear a faint "So do we." echoing after him?

The dogs were ready for the haulage operation and had gone through the final checks before leaving. Mildew had returned to be on call, and Blue and Fleece were still out on their particular assignments.

Tisun, Noodle and Cello were taking stock of the basement area and the stairs leading to it, while King and Tankard checked the entire outside of the building for entrance doors, and also which part could be best seen from the road. The loading bays were round on the right hand side and much of the front was quite plain apart from a small enquiry office, and the name of the firm prominently displayed.

As this was a site totally made up of industrial units, it was easy for the security patrols to get an ample view of most of them without even getting out of their vehicles which some did, whilst the more diligent would go round checking for any sign of tampering, or anything going on that shouldn't be. King had called upon a particularly spiritually aware person in the area to make an anonymous phone call to the police saying they had seen several people lurking near this particular property. As he rang off before giving his name, the police thought it was probably a hoax call, but some people didn't want to get involved for whatever reason and so to be safe they had to check it out. They were told to speak to the security patrol and see if they had noticed anything.

The dogs' senses were now on full alert as a security van pull round the corner. Tisun and the Beagles took the form of illegal immigrants who were running round the building trying to hide. The van stopped and the men hurried towards the images shouting at them to stop but the dogs kept going until they had disappeared near the loading bays. One of the doors appeared to be open slightly and the 'immigrants' were crawling inside.

At that moment a police car arrived with a single officer on board, who, seeing the security men running, got out and followed.

"They've gone in there," one of them shouted but the policeman had seen several others at the far end running round the side of the building.

"There's another lot," he pointed and was about to give chase then stopped. "Can they get in round the back?"

One security man said "Not into here, but they may get into one of the other units."

"I'll go round in the car." As he ran to his vehicle he called for back up as they weren't sure how many individuals were involved. The two security personnel were seeing if they could get in to follow the ones inside but as they were doing so, one noticed a whole group now hovering at the far bay and trying to get in there.

"How the hell are they lifting these doors?" his mate yelled.

"Couldn't have been properly locked. The insurance company are going to love this."

"Not our problem. Where's that copper?"

As if on cue the police car came tearing round the corner his lights now illuminating the people disappearing under the far door but by the time he had got there they were already inside.

"This one's open more, we can get in." he called, so the security men joined him and soon all three were inside.

"Now where do we go?" they asked as it was pitch black and the light of their torches only showed a small area at a time, but wherever they looked there seemed to be bodies scurrying about.

"How many of the bleeders are there?" The policeman asked.

"They must be breeding like rabbits, there's load of them." One replied.

The other cut in "We could be looking at the same ones the way they are flitting around, wish they'd keep bloody still."

"Try and find a light switch." yelled his mate.

Lights outside heralded the arrival of more police, some of whom quickly joined the party inside whist others were checking the surrounding area, but of course they wouldn't find anyone there. As the building lights came on, there were 'immigrants' all over the place but suddenly they seemed to head for one particular area. They ignored all orders to stop and as the officers got near they could see them hurrying down a flight of stairs and out of sight.

The senior police officer instructed his men to proceed with caution, but the new arrivals were well equipped for any eventuality, although nothing prepared them for what they found when they got to the bottom. The clandestines had disappeared completely, but there in full view was the largest cache of arms many of them had seen for a long time. At first they continued the search for the people but having checked every possible hiding place had to accept there was no living soul there.

The dogs hovered over the scene satisfied that their plan had been successful and knew they could now leave the rest to the authorities, although how they would cover losing so many people in their reports would be their problem. Most likely it wouldn't even be mentioned.

The members of the pack were returning to base when King noticed Tankard was missing and asked if he had left without a farewell. For once in a long time Tisun seemed amused.

"Oh, forgot to tell you, he always leaves his trademark."

"Are you saying what I think you're saying?" King was amused now.

"Well nothing physical of course, but he always cocks his leg wherever he goes. Ah, here he comes. Feel better now?" Tisun's mood had lifted considerably.

"Oo ah." was the reply.

Cello said "I've got to ask, why do you do it, I mean there's no need now is there?"

Tisun called over his shoulder "I'll see you all back at base, you'll like this." and he was gone.

"Well?" Noodle couldn't wait to hear this.

"Ah well lad, you sees, when I was living one of my lives down there, in a village, my old master used to walk us down to the pub of an eve'nin. Well they all knew I liked a drop of the local brew, and some used to put a drop of ther'n in a bowl they kept just fer me. Well at the end of the night, I can tell 'ee, I were so pissed I could hardly stand up, let along walk 'ome. Don't ask me 'ow many times I 'ad to cock up before we got there, and as 'e got older, the master couldn't make it either so he used to piss in someone's plants. Well, in 'is memory, I still does one for 'im. Mark of respect like."

King and the Beagles had never come across anyone like this, but they loved this dog and held him in high regard, hoping they would work with him again, because for all his 'old pals' act, they had seen that he was as sharp and sprightly as anyone could be.

As they got to base, Tisun eyed them curiously.

"Well?"

"I told 'em." Tankard laughed in such a way, that apart from Tisun they wondered just how much of the tale had been true, but it didn't matter. Just as he was leaving, Tankard said one word as he passed Tisun and it was only for him to hear. "Mirror."

Chapter 6

The Ladydogs had been kept immobile until it was time for them to return to the school. Raine was very curious about the power of the paws and intended to use the girls to find out just how much of an enemy this unseen force could be to her.

Redhead couldn't wait to get the girls into conference. She drew them to the outside of the building where she knew the paws could protect them, although she didn't know how or why, but her senses were on full alert and she was now following her instinct.

"I know what our bond is." she announced "we are all sisters! We had the same mother but I don't know any more yet."

"How did you work that out?" the quiet one asked.

"It hit my inner self when Raine called us all puny pups."

Without warning the paws gathered the four into their warmth and simultaneously the information was fed to them.

"You are all from the same mother."

Redhead felt herself being pulled upwards. "You were the first from one earth life."

As she was slowly lowered, Dinky and Hannah were raised. "You were born one after the other in another earth life. You first." Dinky was lifted slightly then returned "Then you." The same happened to Hannah. "And you were the dillon of a litter in the most recent earth life, which is why you were referred to as 'the runt'."

The paws gave them a moment for this to sink in and waited for the inevitable question which came from Redhead. "And so we all had different fathers?"

"You will know, when the time is right." and the four were gently released from the comforting euphoria.

"What are you girls doing out here? Didn't you hear the bell?" Miss Clemence's voice cut into their dream world.

"Sorry Miss, we were talking." Hannah hurried forward, but Redhead walked at her own pace, followed as usual by quiet one.

"Get to your class and all of you see me at lunchtime."

Nothing more was said as Dinky hovered over her sisters as they made there way down the corridor.

"So we must all be half sisters," she pondered, "wonder why they didn't tell us. We couldn't possibly all have had the same father, so I don't see what the big secret is." But she was happy to know the connection as were the others, who now had an extra bond which would grow rapidly.

Tisun certainly felt much better after the visit from his friend and he felt his energy flowing back. He was considering calling Mildew off the job at the school, for although they all wanted to know what the paws were, this dog seemed a bit wasted there at present, plus the fact that he was about to be recalled to earth for a tandem stint doing what he did best, searching out bodies. Again Tisun was throwing figures around in his mind. The paws were still grouped apart from the one who appeared to be controlling the others. But what a strange arrangement. Why only two groups? Wouldn't you put your operators at strategic places, not just two, one outside and one in?

"Wait a minute," he thought "perhaps these are at strategic points, so what is special about the staffroom, and that particular wall?" He wasn't paying too much attention to the leader who was distanced from the school, but more in the positioning on the ground. If he had been sitting at a desk he would have been shuffling scribbled notes around in front of him, trying to make sense of it all. But in his mind he was doing just that, all the facts were trying to slot into some sort of pattern and he was sure that something was staring him in the face, shouting at him to look.

He returned to the numbers. Nine and nine, why odd figures, unless each one was three times three, but that didn't make any sense. So including the controller there were nineteen but that drew a blank. His mind raced as though something was steering him. One, nine and nine. Nine, Nine and one. Nine, one nine. Immediately the presence of Tankard's visit was there, reminding him to think, then it hit him.

"Of course. How could I have been so stupid?" But he knew why, because his inner sorrow was still clouding his power to compute the information there in front of him.

"That's why you came here my friend," he breathed and a spiritual tear ran down his handsome face.

Pulling himself together he called Mildew to him. "I have to know what Raine looks like."

"But she never appears, nobody knows."

Tisun put his head to one side quizzically. "Oh No?"

Mildew thought then said "The Ladydogs, they see her."

"Right, get Dinky to tell you, she would be only too pleased to do something for you."

"Hmm. Well alright." Mildew was trying to keep his distance from her as she seemed to have him in her sights and he didn't welcome the increasing enticing vibes she was sending in his direction.

"As soon as you feel like it." Tisun felt he had to give this dog a shove.

"Oh, right now, OK." and he was gone.

It wasn't long before he returned and described Raine as Dinky had very colourfully explained but something wasn't sitting right in the leader's mind.

"I don't think the girls are seeing her as she really is."

"You mean she's feeding them an image to protect her true self." Mildew voiced.

"Not only that, she could have taken it a step further."

"Oh?"

"How do we know that all four of them are seeing the same image?"

"Of course." Mildew had witnessed this tactic before especially in his earth sessions. "And she will show them what she wants them to see, so why is hiding her identity so important?"

"Because if she is who I suspect, she has good reason."

Mildew sat bolt upright. "I've got an idea. Why don't I ask Dinky to check with the others to see how they describe her? That should be interesting." He was very pleased with himself for coming up with the idea but was deflated just as quickly.

"I was wondering how long it would take you." Tisun was back on form now, and nothing was going to stand in his way.

After a short time they had the answer. All the girls' descriptions were different, but now that Mildew had put the thought there, he knew they would all be discussing it at the first opportunity, thus strengthening their bond even further. It came as no surprise to the males that Tisun didn't recognise any of the images as they were manufactured and not the true one.

Raine was getting very frustrated at the incompetence of all the pawns under her control. Clemence for one was useless and she decided to disregard her from now on. If the creature thought she still had a hold on her, well, that was her hard luck. The woman had just lost her mother after a long illness and Raine had threatened that she wouldn't be at peace unless the teacher obeyed the commands. Being quite a timid soul who was physically and mentally drained from the years of caring, hadn't the strength to fight back. She was now free from the evil power's clutches, but sadly was none the wiser, however help was at hand.

She had a free period and was sitting in the staff room her head in her hands feeling utterly drained. Slowly the paws surrounded her and she felt a soothing calmness lift her worries and fears out of her body and soul. Gently the words floated past her.

"You are free. You have nothing to fear. We are here for you all the time. Your mother is safe and free from pain and she just needs to see that you are happy, and says you need a rest. She loves you and thanks you for all you did for her." As the words faded, it was as though they had been stamped upon her permanently, never to be removed and as the truth flooded through her, she fell forward, her head in her hands sobbing from the shear relief of it all. The paws moved upwards knowing she would not turn back now but go forward being herself.

Although Raine had witnessed this little episode, she gave it little consideration. She didn't need the woman anyway and what she did from now on was of little concern and wouldn't stand in the way of her goal.

Next she cast her attention to the bullies. They weren't much better. One did as she was told and the other followed her like a shadow just agreeing with her, but they had achieved little between them. She decided to leave them to whatever fate may befall them as they would never become anything in their own right but were prey for any playful spirit looking for trouble.

Clemence walked into the classroom for the next lesson her head high and with a new purpose. The four girls noticed the change immediately and Hannah almost breathed a sigh of relief, but they were all rather suspicious wondering if this was a new tactic

"Hannah will you take these forms round and give them out please?" she was actually smiling, but before there was a reply Redhead rose to her feet and put her hand on Hannah's shoulder, forcing her into her seat.

"It's alright Miss, Hannah's not feeling well, I'll do it." then turning to her sister said loud enough for all to hear "you're not going to be sick again are you?"

"Sick, she's been sick?" Clemence looked horrified but Redhead calmly replied "That's why we took her outside earlier, we were going to tell you when we came to the staff room."

"Well, are you alright now?" the teacher asked Hannah.

"I think so, thank you Miss."

Redhead took the forms and made sure her back was to Miss Clemence as she made her way through the desks. To every other pupil apart from the bullies she whispered "Dee is a les." Before long the whole class was giggling and pointing at the two and although order was called for the humour had gathered momentum and various unsavoury comments were being hurled in their direction. That should have been enough for any mischief maker, but the sisters had a score to settle and weren't going to leave it there. The quiet one sat unmoved by all the fracas, but when she felt the time was right, all the mobile phones started to ring at once as if a starting pistol had gone off and yet her face showed no emotion. To add to her innocence, she also took out hers so that nobody would remotely think she had anything to do with it.

This latest spate of defiance was giving the girls more and more power by the minute which didn't go unnoticed by Raine.

"I've got to change my plans" she decided. Originally she wanted to dispose of them one by one reaping the satisfaction along the way, but things weren't going her way. She knew the paws were playing a big part in it but dare not try to find out who or what they were and why they were here now.

If the girls were gathering strength that could be used against her, she must use their power to her own advantage to draw her target into the web. Now she was going straight for Tisun, and nothing would stand in her way. Pippa had taken him from her, or at least got him before she had a chance and it was now time to get even. She knew it wouldn't be an easy task for he wouldn't just fall into her clutches, she would have to work on him but in a subtle way until he couldn't resist her, and she would use any underhand means she could until he couldn't escape. It never occurred to her ego that there is no reward in having somebody that doesn't want you in return, for she firmly believed that by the time she had finished with him, he would love her as he had loved Pippa.

She had been so angered by the love he held for someone that should have been her, that she had employed evil entities to despatch Pippa far out into the unknown to travel aimlessly for evermore, but letting everyone think that she had the power to do it. When Ruby had stepped in to protect the daughters, Raine had repeated the operation and now she had complete control using her reign of fear.

So now she would get them to draw Tisun to her. He must be wondering by now who was in control, for after all, they were all his daughters, and if he hadn't worked it out by now, he soon would.

Most of the male dogs were back at base summing up their recent results and Mildew was relating the effect the paws had on him, when the order came for him to go to Vancouver Island in Canada and start his tandem stint.

"Oh not now," was his first reaction but Tisun reminded him he wouldn't be tied to one body, but be able to flit back and forth within reason.

"As long as you learn any new tricks while you are there, that's all that matters."

"But what about the school?" Mildew moaned.

"Ha, he wants to go back for another fix," Blue knew what the objection was but couldn't resist adding, "unless it's that little bitch who fancies you."

"No thank you."

"Alright boys, let's keep it together," Tisun knew that there was no option regarding his friend but knew he may have to regroup, especially at this crucial time for he knew things would be hotting up now.

"Thought I'd just pop in. You going then?" The familiar drawl brightened up the entire area.

"Tankard" was the chorus from all except the leader who eyed him with friendly suspicion.

"Now that's a coincidence, or is it?" he greeted his pal.

"Well I says to them upstairs that me mate might be glad of an 'and just now and if they 'ad no objection like, I might as well wander over and see if you can use I."

"I don't mind so much now, seeing that you're in such good hands." Mildew brightened up.

When an order comes from the higher powers, it means it is carried out without delay so Mildew's parting had to be very quick and moments after Tankard's unexpected appearance he left for Canada.

"Well carry on, don't mind me." Tankard urged them to get on with the matters in hand. Although Tisun started to explain the current situation at the school he had the uncanny feeling that this dog knew all about it, possibly even more then he did.

"Suppose I goes and takes a gander at it, casual like?" he continued.

Tisun was weighing up the pros and cons. He would love to go himself but suspected a trap, and Raine may not find this dog a threat as he could give the appearance of an old soul wandering about and who just happened to be passing. But what if she knew him?

The others had gone back to their various jobs now and the two buddies were alone.

Tankard was the first to speak. "You worked it out then?"

"Somewhat. And thank you for the clue, it took a while but now it makes sense. But you can understand I have had to clear it from my mind."

"Course you 'ave. Don't want them picking up on your thoughts. And now you're wondering who the head bitch is." He eyed him knowingly.

"There can only be one. But I've got to prove it and she isn't showing her hand to anyone."

"Aha. Well she aint 'ad me to contend with yet."

Tisun looked him straight on. "You old dog. You're not here by chance, you never were. I'm right aren't it?"

95

If he expected any form of a positive reply he was disappointed but he knew his friend too well and didn't press it any further.

"So I'll be off then." He got up and was gone almost before Tisun could wish him luck.

Chapter 7

PC Soames was back on duty and Radar was glad to be at work. He often wished he had the total freedom of his spiritual friends but they all had to do their stints in the physical world. King was in the area and placed himself in the back of the dog van with him, soon exchanging notes on their recent activities.

"Felt as though I was retired." Radar joked "Not like you."

"Well as soon as we finish one, there's always another, and mine seems to be on the increase."

"Funny you should say that," Radar was thoughtful, "could you have a look at something for me?"

"Course. What is it?"

They were travelling along the road past the warehouse that had been the site of the handprint activity but was now completely clean.

"There." Radar indicated. "Been lot of strange things going on there."

"Oh we heard about the shooting, and those strange prints, but we were told to back off, unofficially you understand."

"Well, there's still something, I just know it."

King paused "I'd better have a word with boss man, he was very insistent we kept away, mind you that was before it got cleansed. Perhaps it's alright now and he is a bit tied up with something going on at a school."

"Can you come when I'm asleep, we could go together?"

"Don't see why not. Shouldn't hurt."

They agreed to meet later when Radar's body was sleeping and find out for themselves what was going on.

Dinky had been summoned, which meant that Raine wanted her at base now.

"I want you to get that friend of yours to bring his leader, there's something I want to discuss with him."

"Well, I can only ask, I mean I don't know if he will come or not." Dinky wasn't trembling in her presence even if she was on her own without backup.

"Don't get cocky, if I say bring him, I mean bring him."

"Well I'll do my best."

Raine's face was inches from her. "It had better be, or else."

Dinky was so tempted to say "or else what" but stopped and gave the leader a hard stare before she left. Actually she was delighted to have a good reason to approach Mildew the next time he appeared and she felt a pang of disappointment that he had been away so long. He had flitted to and fro before, but this time it seemed like ages and she missed him.

She located the other girls and related the conversation.

"Hmm, wonder what the witch is up to now." Redhead was first to jump in.

"I don't trust her." Hannah agreed while the quiet one just nodded in agreement.

"Well as soon as he gets back I will tell him." Dinky thought.

"Can't you get a message to him?" Redhead said suddenly, "You know, like you did when he first came."

There was a pause. "I didn't actually do it myself, somebody did it for me."

"What?" All three were looking at her.

Redhead looked her straight on. "Ok. What happened? All of it now."

Dinky looked embarrassed as she started "Well, I know we, or rather you were put here because of the bullying, but it didn't seem to add up. So I was thinking that we could do with a bit of help and this person came by...."

"Just a minute, what person came by where?" Hannah didn't like the sound of this.

"I'm telling you. I was thinking.....and suddenly an old dog was there and said he knew someone who could help me and all I had to do was wish it."

"Oh my stars, what are we going to do with you?" Redhead almost exploded.

Quiet one spoke softly "And you believed him?"

"Well yes, he was nice and he wanted to help and I couldn't see the harm. You all agreed things weren't as they seem and now we know they aren't."

"So where is this Mildew chap now? Seems to have got fed up if you ask me." Redhead was on the defensive

"Look." Quiet one was pointing to the grass beyond the playground.

"Oh some dog's got in and having a piss." Redhead didn't want to be distracted but Dinky almost yelled. "That's him."

"Tell me I'm imagining it," Hannah said "you're not going to tell us he got Mildew here are you?"

Dinky didn't know where to put herself. This tatty old dog was prowling around cocking its leg on anything it could find, but was now making its way down by the side of the building where the paws were hovering.

"Well this should be amusing" Redhead laughed, "let's see if he pisses up them."

"What are you girls making all the fuss about?" The sound of their next teacher entering the room made them jump.

"Um -we thought we saw a dog Miss." Hannah ventured.

"Dog, what dog?" the woman came to the window, "I can't see anything. Now go to your places."

The class took their places but Dinky hovered near the window but there was no sign of anything moving and it seemed as though he had disappeared. Thinking he may have come to offer help again, she drifted out of the building and stayed near the paws.

"Thought you come out 'ere." The voice made her jump.

"It was you. Have you come to tell me why Mildew isn't here?"

"Quick little thing aren't you?" He eyed her up. "You taken a fancy to 'im, aint you?"

"Well, he is nice. And he's big isn't he?"

"Ooh ah, 'es a biggun alright."

"Do you know why he's been so long?"

Tankard sat down. "Look 'ere now, there's lots going on besides this place. He's got another job to do."

"Oh." Dinky was only thinking of her own disappointment when Raine's order hit her."Oh no, he can't."

Tankard looked interested. "And why might that be then?"

"Um I can't say."

"Ah. I see, got your orders 'ave you?" He saw the look on her face and added "Why don't you just get along and leave it to me?"

"She probably knows I'm talking to you."

"Well let me tell you, she can't"

"Wh..at?" Dinky was curious as to the powers of this dog.

"Oh there's a lot she don't know."

Dinky was really puzzled now, he seemed to be talking in riddles then she realised that they were encased in one of the sets of paws and the idea came to her that these were acting as a protection and even Raine couldn't penetrate their force field.

He looked at her kindly "You come 'ere whenever you wants. Private place so to speak."

"Thank you I will." She felt at ease now and didn't want to leave this safe haven as though it belonged to her alone and she suddenly realised he had gone but she had no idea where.

Raine may have been able to fool the sisters by masking her true appearance but there were those of a much superior power who could see right through the facade. Tisun was one, but he would not show his hand until he was certain, but Tankard wandered around attracting little attention as he was quite a familiar figure, so nobody thought he was going anywhere in particular.

Within the space of about two seconds he had located the Ladydog base, flown across it and scanned Raine and returned to Tisun.

"Well?" the leader was eager to know.

"Oh it's 'er alright. Saw through 'er like a pane o'glass."

Tisun uttered one word "Helga."

"That's the one. And she be after you."

He brought him up to date regarding the girls, confirming they were all ok with their energy being charged by the paws.

"Well that's one good thing at least, and I know where they are. I was afraid she might have despatched them the same way as......" he cleared his mind again so that no thoughts could travel but his friend knew what he meant. He also didn't have to explain that he knew he was the father of them all, albeit from different earth visits, but now the game took on a different perspective.

The comrades remembered the years of jealousy that had festered inside Helga and the ensuing rage that had been aimed at them all through not only their earth lives, but their continual spiritual existence. She had turned the space around them into a living hell and thought she could still get what she wanted with hatred, fear and power. Her sort never realise that instead of drawing people nearer, there are in fact driving them further away and burning all their bridges in the process. She had been keen to let Tisun know that she had despatched his beloved for good followed by her sister and when she had finished with his offspring she would be only too happy to let them go the same way, to wander aimlessly for eternity. She never imagined that the truth might come out and she could be exposed as a liar and someone not to be feared but despised.

Tisun knew by instinct that Tankard had full knowledge of the message being sent by the paws, as he had given him the clue. The formation of 9 1 9 mirrored read P I P, but he dare not show his gratitude and both were wiping it from their thoughts so that no trace could be monitored by Helga. It was obvious the paws were either protecting her elsewhere, or she was nearby but that was unlikely at this stage. Now he was on full steam, driven by the inner feeling of being reunited but he let his anger and feeling of disgust take over to mask such emotions. Now they two set about planning their next move.

King waited for Radar to settle and was surprised when they were joined by Jack.

"Where are you two off? Thought you'd go without me did you?" he laughed.

"Didn't think you were in sleep yet." Radar looked disappointed.

"That's obvious."

"Oh well, as you're here you might as well tag along," King laughed "but be careful, we're not entirely sure we should be nosing around there."

"Lead on." Jack indicated for the dogs to go in front and soon they were watching the warehouse from a distance.

"See what I mean?" Radar was on full alert pose.

"Will you take a look at that?" Jack's mouth dropped open, even though he was not in body.

Above them, small lights seemed to be leaving the building and floating heavenwards, not in any pattern, just here and there, some in groups but some solitary ones which looked quite lonely.

"Let's go nearer." Radar was already moving but King paused.

"Take it slowly we don't know what this is. I've never seen anything quite like it before."

As they got nearer to the warehouse they realised that the lights weren't coming from there at all but much further back. They instinctively looked at each other wondering what was going on, and started to move as one being towards the source.

"So the warehouse is clean?" King sounded relieved knowing he hadn't broken any previous rules.

"Have you noticed," Jack felt he had to whisper, "we are moving but don't seem to be getting any closer."

"As though it's moving away at our pace." Radar paused then shot forward quickly to see if this was the case. "Come on, I think it's stopped." he called.

Gingerly they moved as one until they felt rather than saw something in front of them. If it had been physical, the best way to describe it, would be that a door opened and someone welcomed them in to an area where they would witness something they would never forget again.

"Come my friends," the message was warm and caring and the three felt themselves floating into a protected area.

"Where are we?" King was the first to ask.

"And what is this place?" Radar added.

The person's image was of a nursing nun but she was not alone. As they became accustomed to the place, they realised it was filled with such people but what were they tending?

"It take's a bit of understanding, and not many experience this work we do, but you are welcome, you seem kindly souls." She indicated for them to move further along the rows which were appearing as they looked. Every so often one of the lights they had seen earlier rose up and left an empty space beneath it as it travelled upwards and out of sight.

"Bless you," the nun whispered as it left.

The two dogs and Jack weren't sure if they really wanted to know what was going on here but their curiosity took over.

"Are they little aliens?" Radar sniffed the air.

The nun laughed "Not exactly but I can see why you may think that. Just a moment please." She left them as a group of lights travelled upwards but their spaces were immediately filled with newcomers and a tremendous feeling of sadness crept over the area. Making sure they were comforted by other nurses, the nun came back.

"I'm sorry, it's always like this."

The three visitors were now aware that the area seemed to be extending as far as it was possible to see and wondered why they hadn't noticed it before.

"Would you like me to explain?" she asked and when they agreed she added "but I must warn you, it may be very upsetting, it is to some people although others seem to take comfort by our work."

"Well as we are here now, we may as well." King looked at his friends for confirmation and they both nodded.

"Very well." Their guide moved them to a place just away from the patients. "This is where the souls are brought who are not ready to move on or as often described, earthbound."

"But there are so many." King was astounded at the new arrivals coming in constantly.

"Sadly yes. But we know they are peaceful when they have left us and they can then progress at their normal pace."

"So these are the results of say, murders or traffic accidents, that kind of thing?" Jack was scanning the ones nearest to him and they all seemed so young.

"They can be of course, any sudden wrenching of the soul, but there are many not like that."

"Can you tell us?" King had heard of such places but never seen one.

"With pleasure. Some people are ready to go at whatever age as they know they will go back to being in total spirit. Some are even glad to loose their earthly trappings and regain their freedom. Some are so wrapped up in their earthly lives, they will not break the tie and move on."

"So you help them?" Jack was fascinated.

"Someone has to, or they would never be released. Let me explain. They think they will be closer to their loved ones if they

103

remain but that isn't the case. They have to go through the transition essential to their future progress, and when they have achieved that, then they can come and communicate with those able to receive their messages."

"You try and explain this to them?" Jack thought this was obvious but had to ask.

"Of course, but it isn't that easy. How many times have you tried to advise someone in your job, but they thought they knew best."

"Oh, hundreds, and some will never change. Ah, what am I saying?"

"I think you've just answered your own question." she laughed.

Radar was pondering. "What about those who seem to have left their bodies before they are actually dead?"

"Now you are onto a different area. They don't come here, in fact it's a job to get them to transit at a sensible pace, they're in such a hurry to meet Auntie Maud or whoever." Again her tone wasn't sombre but quite light hearted.

"Hey look," Radar was pointing, "there's dogs and cats and what's that?"

"Oh we get all kinds of life, spirits aren't confined to humans as you are very well aware."

"Oh I know that, but they're all mixed up. Look, there's a bloody giraffe" he looked as far as he could see, "there's everything all together."

Jack cut in "OK boy, we see them. What the sister is trying to say is that everything living has a soul, and when it moves from one state to another it has to go through another door so to speak. They all do."

"My word Jack," the sister was very impressed, "when you are totally in spirit, can we offer you a job. I don't think you'd need much training."

He visibly took a step back. "Woah, hang on, I'm not quite ready for that yet thanks."

She looked at him very deeply as she whispered "Then it's a good job that bullet only grazed you isn't it?"

That brought the truth of it all home and hit him in the face. Anyone could be snatched at a moments' notice and then how would they cope with the sudden fact that they were, to put it in human terms, dead? Even the dogs were brought to a halt. They had been looking at the 'casualties' as them, not us. These were not different, they were just others in whatever form that were not coping with change and they had to be helped through it, much as the earthly beings had to be helped through illness and bereavement.

They all remained silent as they watched the lucky ones rising and could now see the helpers taking their souls to their next level.

"Is this the only place like it, it's so overcrowded?" Radar was looking around.

"Oh no, there are more but usually nobody comes across them, we try to keep them away from the main track."

The lights were ascending at quite a pace now and everyone felt a tremendous sense of achievement, but the empty places were filled straight away.

"This may not seem like a quiet area to choose," the nun continued, but we had rather a spate of it round here so had to accommodate them as quickly as possible. Hopefully we can close it soon if the demand dies down."

"We certainly are seeing a different aspect," Jack was still fascinated.

The nun smiled. "You will understand that areas such as this are not on general view. Most people would be very unwell merely at the sight of it." The nun still had her mind on what was going on in front of her.

"Even in the physical sense it would make a few puke that I know." Radar was still amazed by the enormity of it and was transfixed by the lights which were still rising. "Is there someone waiting for them when they get there?"

"Yes, our helpers have done their job so they hand them onto the next ones to take over."

"Don't think I could do it." Jack said, "Not as a job."

The nun laughed, "You don't know what you can do until the time comes, you've met with a few nasty ones, I can tell."

"Well I suppose, but you just get on with it. Ah I get your point." He was forced to smile.

They had all just about had enough when King suggested they leave and let these good people get on with their work.

"Thank you for caring, "the nun said, then added "glad your arm is better Jack."

They returned to Jack's house in silence then all seemed to start talking at once.

"Bloody hell fire!"

"I never expected that."

"Thought you were going to be sick."

Radar mused "We don't know the half of what goes on do we? We think we do, but there's more up there...."

"...and down here mate" Jack cut in. "We'll never know it all. What are you going to tell your boss?"

King thought for a moment. Then said defiantly "The truth. Why not?" Then pausing he faced them, "You know, I still think that business with the warehouse had something to do with it. Maybe souls were being interfered with from there."

"Bit extreme if it was to cover up a mass soul despatch." Jack pointed out.

"Depends what was involved." Radar was getting ready to return to his body, and as Jack did the same, King left them with the thought "We will probably never know."

"So," Tisun mused "it's me she's after, so...."

"Let's give 'er what she wants?" Tankard finished the sentence eying his friend, then added "You up to it?"

"More than ever, and what's more, she may have thought she ruled supreme up till now, but is she in for a surprise?"

"Ponder this." Tankard was looking far away now. "You wants to protect them lasses o' yours."

"Well of course I do. They need me."

"Ha, I shouldn't be so sure o' that lad."

Tisun stood up. "What do you mean by that?"

"Calm down and listen."

When his mate had resumed his position Tankard said very slowly "They aren't as feeble as you dads likes to think. They got some spike they 'ave. You could do a lot worse than 'ave 'em on your side." He pulled back watching the change in Tisun as the truth sank in.

"We all fight her together?"

"Well now, you thinking fer yerself at last." There was a sly amusement on his face. Then he added, "Course you might be glad of a bit of a nudge 'ere an' there. I mean someone 'as to pop down an' tell 'em, and you can't."

"Well Mildew… oh he's got that other thing hasn't he?"

There was a silence then Tisun stood right up. "You canny old dog. You've been planning this all along haven't you?"

"Me?"

"Ok, Ok, let's sort out what we are going to do."

It didn't take long for the leader to realise he should have had his wits about him before this, but without dwelling on that too much he knew he was on full steam now and this plan would work. After a fairly short discussion and almost without a farewell, Tankard had gone to sow the seeds.

Raine or rather Helga, had been working out the best way to make Tisun want to come to her. She had enough sense to know that he wouldn't just walk into her lair once he knew who she really was, so she had to act before he found out, and due to her cleverness that wasn't about to happen as she hadn't shown her true self to any around her. The obvious plan was to use the girls to get him to show his hand but that seemed to have fallen flat because the creature that Dinky had the hots for didn't seem to be around so she would have to think of another way.

But something was niggling at the back of her mind. Why hadn't he attempted to visit? But she dismissed that with another proverbial pat on her back. It hadn't seemed important enough for one so lofty as he, and he had merely sent one of his underlings to sort the bullying not realising the connection with his pups, so all was well. With Mildew's apparent disinterest, it did present the problem that the connections were being severed with the dog pack, so she felt she was starting from square one again. The girls were tiresome, but she couldn't risk letting them out of her clutches as they seemed the only lead. Then, out of sheer desperation she thought she had now found the answer. Let him know her identity, but let him think the girls were in danger of being despatched, which was her original idea.

Everything seemed to be so against her, it now occurred to her that there must be another force interfering with her plans, so that every time she tried something else, it was squashed.

"The paws things. It has to be those blasted paw...whatever they are. They are at the bottom of this." She screamed until the air around her shook with anger. "Everything was going fine until they showed up. Well I'll show them."

Being fully aware she couldn't possibly do it alone she was forced to consider calling on help from the evil power that had despatched Pippa and Ruby. She didn't know who it was, but she knew how to summon it although it did have the down side. It would give her the power when she asked for it, but she in turn would ultimately have to dance to their tune. This had never bothered her before as she lived for now and only thought of the control she had over people when she needed it, not realising it could be snatched away as quickly. It was rather like having a credit card, it answered her problems for the time being but she was now so heavily in debt, it was doubtful if she would ever be able to pay it back.

But this was something it was worth paying heavily for. She would have her love, the one that should have been hers and it didn't matter what it cost to get him.

Although he felt guilty admitting it, Mildew was rather enjoying the break away from the boring situation at the school. Nothing seemed to be moving along very much and he was the constant object of adoration from Dinky. The only spark of enjoyment recently had been his association with the paws, and he would like to have pursued that further, but guessed that by the time he got back they would have left the place.

He was in tandem with Butch who seemed to be a dog of his own temperament, and soon the two were working as one. They discussed the individual jobs they had encountered in their various lives, but the details of how and where they found the bodies is best left to their own knowledge.

Now they were in the back of a vehicle heading north on Vancouver Island to where a young lady had last been seen and to start the job from there. Being back in his own special field, Mildew wasn't in any hurry to return to base, and certainly not until this job had been satisfactorily resolved. The two were now concentrating their minds on finding the remains wherever they were, and in whatever state.

The Ladydogs were now visiting the paws on a regular basis, feeling their strength building. The quiet one had suggested that it might be a good idea to go separately thus not drawing so much attention to themselves, as it may seen strange if they all disappeared at once.

"You are always the thinker," Redhead laughed but could see the sense in the idea. Miss Clemence may have stopped her bullying tactics for whatever reason, but they were aware she still had her beady eye on them, especially when they were altogether. Also they decided to vary the times so that no pattern appeared to be forming.

Hannah was still edgy as she didn't know quite how to act. The meek character was fading but she felt she had no purpose.

"I feel has though we are hanging around for nothing when we could be out doing our normal jobs." she voiced.

"Well I'm fed up here now." Dinky almost pouted

"Because your handsome prince isn't here." Redhead laughed but her sister didn't find it very amusing.

"I think we are here for a reason." The quiet one only spoke when she had something sensible to offer and the rest tended to listen but asked her to explain.

"I believe we were brought here to be ready when something happened."

"What?" was the chorus.

"If I knew that……" she paused "let's just say, I've been keeping my eye on people and I think we should be very careful."

"What people are we talking about? Anyone in particular?" Redhead was getting interested.

The quiet one's head turned in the direction of Clemence.

"No. Really?" Redhead questioned.

"Everything may not be as it appears, I'm sure of it."

There was a moment's silence as everyone mulled over this latest idea. They had thought she was a bully, but then that didn't tie up because away from the school she was like a terrified little mouse.

"Have you been watching anyone else?" Dinky wondered.

"A few, but I always come back to her for some reason."

"Wow." Hannah brightened up, "just when I thought it was getting boring. Oh, I want to stay around now and see what happens. You know, I never did trust her."

"Ok ladies" Redhead called for order. "Let's not get carried away. Got any proof?"

"Not as yet, "the quiet one answered but looked as though she knew something but was keeping it to herself for now, "as soon as I do, you will know."

"Fair enough then." Redhead said. "Well, I'm off for my daily fix."

The Ladydogs were getting so accustomed to this procedure that they only had to be out of human view and think 'paws' and they were there in an instant. Although they were used to this, today seemed different.

"My God you were in a hurry." Redhead's humour always sent a tremble of amusement through the group but where was it now? She was very quick to pick up on this and before she could question it, the thought was planted into her mind.

"Be careful."

She had enough sense to know this would not be an idle warning.

"What of?"

"Stay very alert" was the next message.

"Are we in danger?"

"The worst kind."

This last part silenced Redhead for a moment.

"Can you tell me more please?"

"Watch, listen, be aware of everything, trust nothing."

"I need to know."

There was silence but the warmth closed round her so tightly she felt it would crush her. Slowly it released her and she found herself back in the school, but something had been implanted which caused her to tread very carefully and she felt an increasing distrust of all around her. For some reason she decided not to tell the others just yet and see if they too received the same message when they went for their session. It would be interesting to find out if they were all told the same or got different messages.

Tankard had finished his preparations and Tisun, knowing this boy of old couldn't resist joking "We can all guess the kind of seeds you've been sowing you dirty old hound."

"Ah, not this time, had more important things to plant."

"If you say so." The humour covered the seriousness of the job to come.

"You ready for this?"

Tisun checked that King was around while the others were out on calls then said "Bring it on."

"Right. The school's finished for the weekend, so the girls have gone back to the base."

As prearranged, Tankard left the base for his own vantage point leaving Tisun to move at a certain time.

Helga was chastising the females, more to keep her air of authority than for any other reason. She was about to explain what she wanted them to do when a disturbance in the air attracted her attention.

"What the hell is that at the school?" she exploded.

"Shall we go and see Miss?" Redhead's sarcasm only fuelled the anger.

"Wait. I don't believe it." Helga was watching the form hovering above the school and it was facing her, getting clearer by the minute. "It can't be!"

Without a second thought she flew to the image. "Tisun you came."

The unblinking eyes stared right through her as he sat erect like a king on his throne. There was something in his expression that made her slow down until she was a few feet from him.

"Why have you come?" she asked feebly.

"Isn't that what you have been planning?" was the low growl of a reply.

"Well, yes, of course, but I didn't expect......"

"....that I would come to you."

His eyes were like flames burning into her as he finished the sentence for her. She was almost paralysed in his presence as she never expected it to be like this.

"I could have come at any time."

111

"But you didn't know who I was." She was wondering now how long he had known and he wasn't going to let her off this lightly.

"Oh really. And what makes you think that?"

She was floundering now. All her plans seemed to be evaporating and she was trying hard to find a suitable reply.

"In fact you should think yourself very lucky." he continued "The hatred I have nurtured could have destroyed you at any time."

"B..b..but I used another image. How could you have known?"

There was a long pause before he said very precisely "You think you are clever Helga, but you are nothing. You have only the power you pay for. You have ruled the girls with fear when all the time they could have taken you out of the picture. But of course they will know now, so that should be rather interesting don't you think?"

"This isn't you." She was spluttering, grasping for life lines. "Don't you think I'd know the man of my dreams. You are an impostor. I could never have loved you."

"You didn't. You stalked, you wanted to possess, to own. No Helga, you didn't want love, you don't know how to love."

The words hit her like arrows and suddenly all the past feelings turned to utter hatred. She flew at him with all the force she could muster, calling on the evil power to help her destroy him for good by sending him along the same route as Pippa and Ruby.

He held her back with a force while he laughed "You didn't send them anywhere. You were conned Helga. You paid for jobs that weren't done."

"No." she screamed until the air trembled around them. "You are lying. They went and they can never come back."

"Oh I wouldn't be too sure of that my dear." His words were sour.

"You can't prove it!" she had the sudden inspiration that if he was playing with her, he had just slipped up.

"Alright you win." The words came as a shock and although she was delighted to hear them, the pleasure was short lived for he beckoned to his right side and out of a mist floated the most beautiful white German Shepherd one could imagine.

Her reply was choked "It can't be. I sent her away."

"And Ruby too?" he asked as another image appeared on his left side.

"No! This is a trick, it can't be them."

As Tisun, flanked by the two beauties slowly faded away his words echoed "Oh no trick Helga, this is for real."

She was a solitary figure. All the years of waiting and planning to get him for herself came crashing down around her and all she could feel was devastation. But someone had to be blamed, and who was the nearest in the line of fire? The girls. Quickly she returned to base but it was empty. For one horrible moment she thought they may have been watching her torment but there was no sign of them anywhere in the surrounding area. She called them by name but the silence was her only answer. They must have gone wandering off somewhere she thought, but knew there had to be more to it than that. Frantically she scanned the school, hovering near the paws, but all was still.They couldn't all have gone out on a task, because she hadn't sent them.

It was the last part of the sentence that made her realise the truth. They didn't have to be ruled by her any more, they were free to go where they pleased, with or without her consent. In other words she had lost her hold and her reign was over. But the likes of Helga refuse to be beaten and mask the truth by creating possible answers instead of facing the inevitable.

"Just wait till they come back," she fumed "they have a lesson to learn."

"But you will have a long wait" was the thought coming from Tisun as he returned to base, alone.

Tankard wasn't far behind him. "Well?"

"I don't know how we did it. It was hard." Tisun was trying to stay strong after being so close to even the image of Pippa. "But I have to hand it to you, you were damned good."

"Not lost me touch then?"

Eager not to loose face and dwell on the happenings, Tisun asked when they would make the next move and why Pippa couldn't be returned now as Helga was under the impression that she had been.

"Not quite that simple." Tankard was obviously hiding something.

"Can't you tell me?" Tisun looked determined and his friend knew it was time to divulge the facts or this dog wouldn't rest and may hamper the outcome.

Taking a deep breath he began.

"Let's go through it from the start. Helga got some evil force to send Pippa and then Ruby off course so that they would travel aimlessly in space for ever, and if that had happened, there is nothing any power could have done to bring them back. Well when you employ rubbish, you get rubbish. In earthly terms, they took her payment but didn't come up with the goods. They were both intercepted by the good lot and taken to a safe place where no one could find them. Been there ever since."

Tisun was so engrossed that he hadn't noticed his friend had dropped his country drawl and was explaining in very fluent speech.

He asked "And so they are still there now?"

"Course they are. I had a good look so I could get the images right. Quite pleased with myself on that one, I must say."

"So let's get this straight. You can go and see them, but I can't."

"That's about it."

"Why?"

"Think about it lad."

"Because you are an expert at shape shifting and nobody bothers when you are shuffling around like a homeless mongrel, like you are now for that matter." It was then it hit him. "You're speaking differently."

Tankard gave the impression of a dog grin, lifting one lip up to show a few teeth. "Go on."

Tisun was being pushed to ask the next question. "What do you really look like?"

"Well that doesn't come into it. Let's get back to Helga, and the ladies. Yes they are being very well looked after and they want to get back, but it's not the right time yet."

"Hang on." Tisun looked suspicious. "You're not using them as bait? Please tell me you're not doing that?"

"No, not in so many words."

"Perhaps you had better tell me in what words."

Tankard paused for a moment then continued. "They aren't being dangled like a maggot to catch a fish, but the fact they aren't here is making certain forces think they are in control."

"Well we know she isn't" referring to Helga.

"Oh not her. She's nothing, except she did prove it worked, so she was a good test case."

"You were using her!"

"Well, she didn't have many more uses did she?" he laughed.

"And what about my girls?" Tisun was anxious to be reunited with them too.

"Ah yes, the girls. Well Helga had planned to despatch them as well, but that could never have happened as you can imagine. But they are still in the play at the moment. Can't pull them yet."

"You're controlling them as well? I don't believe this. What use can they be? I'm not being unkind but they aren't dog pack calibre. Yes they do a lot of good but only in a small way." Tisun was feeling there was something a lot more sinister going on and he hadn't been privy to it. But he wanted to know everything now. This was his family they were discussing.

"You couldn't know everything, your mind had to be ignorant of it or they would have picked up on your vibes."

"Who's 'they'? I kept Pippa out of my thoughts because of Helga. Are you saying it wasn't her that was the threat?"

"I'm saying exactly that."

"Then who in creation is it?" not getting a reply he added "You aren't going to tell me are you?"

"It isn't a case of not telling you, it more that you wouldn't understand. There are levels of existence that would blow your mind. Things that are done you wouldn't believe. Now, when we come up against situations such as these, there are special ways of dealing with them, but only by those in the know."

"And you are, aren't you, in the know I mean?"

"We don't need to go into that. Just leave it to those who can fight the very evil forces, because believe me you just wouldn't understand what it takes."

It was quite a while before they communicated again but Tisun was worried that the girls could be in danger.

"They will be very well protected, have no fear on that score." Tankard assured him.

"The paws."

There was no affirmation, just the hint of acknowledgement.

"So where do we go from here?" Tisun new it was a futile question.

"We don't. There is nothing more you can do apart from carry on and give the impression all is just the same." When he saw the disappointment on his friend's face, Tankard said "At least you now know the ladies are safe and not gone forever, so take comfort in that, and your girls are near and will remain so. Keep your distance, think of their safety, and don't do anything out of the norm."

"I will." Although it was a reluctant reply, Tisun knew this was how it had to be for now, in order to achieve the end result.

Chapter 8

It was time for taking stock in many areas. Although Tisun's mind was full of recent revelations, he knew his duty was still to oversee the pack, and as everyone apart from Mildew seemed to be temporarily between jobs, now seemed a good time to catch up.

Fleece was first to offer his contribution and at first the others wondered why he was bothering to tell the same old tale, but it soon became apparent that this was not the run of the mill. He had been called to another care home for the elderly but with a difference. The daughter of one of the residents always noticed that she seemed to be short of money whenever she had visited the place and felt she had to report it to the manager who said she would look into it.

The lady's mother was a quiet little soul, and the question arose as to whether the money left with her had also been taken. This threw suspicion on the members of staff who were all questioned, but then it seemed that they too had found money was missing from their bags left in their locker room. Now the manager was looking at the possibility of visitors going round helping themselves while the residents were at lunch or being washed. The rooms were not locked, although the doors were closed when the rooms were empty, with the exception of the domestics who had the doors wide open whilst they were cleaning and the carers when the beds were being made.

So it was time to turn to the cameras and see just what was going on. What it proved was beyond belief. The quiet little mother often liked a little walk down the corridor and nobody took much notice of her apart from the odd pleasantries. She had it timed to the second. When her daughter had nipped down to speak to the manager, she had dipped her fingers into her bag which had been left near her in the room. She knew when the staff left the locker room, and as they often left their stuff lying around, there was plenty to choose from. Visitors were an easy picking as they didn't always carry their things around with them, and she knew very well which residents were bed ridden, and those that would be taken down for lunch leaving their rooms unattended. She could make her own way to the dining room and often was the last to arrive so nobody gave that a thought.

The manager called the daughter in and showed her the footage so that she could be present when the room was searched. But this old lady was canny and looked perfectly calm and not bothered about them going through her belongings. They found money stuffed into all sorts of places and wondered why they hadn't discovered it before. She didn't need it to spend, she just liked having it as in her youth the family hadn't been very well off and now she could own lots of it, just to possess it.

They had to question her, but she played the 'don't remember doing it' act and who could prove otherwise so they decided to deal with it themselves and not bring in the authorities. The daughter felt that the reason she had taken the money was proof enough that there was some sort of mental problem, and to address that side of it.

"Fascinating story Fleece," Blue said, "but where did you come in?"

"Well you don't think they worked it out by themselves do you?"

"So?" Blue wasn't letting him get away with it and sensed that Fleece was hiding something.

"Well...."

"Yes?" they all chorused.

"For a start I'd seen what the lady was doing apart from smelling where it all was. Then I followed her, sprightly lass she was too I can tell you, popping in and out of rooms, helping herself then back to her own place."

"Go on." They still felt he was stalling.

"You know that we have to give things a shove now and again. And I knew they would look at the cameras eventually."

"Here it comes, and not before time." Blue was almost sarcastic.

Fleece gave him one of his "Do you mind?" looks and continued. "Well they looked at the camera footage and saw all they needed to see. It was all there."

Now Blue knew. "And they didn't even query why they were looking at things that were out of camera view?"

"Really, were they?" Fleece couldn't have looked more innocent if he had tried.

"You did the quick flash, enough to see her doing things you'd seen and were imaging on the monitor, and they didn't even notice."

"Perhaps it was something of that nature." Fleece's reply brought forth a round of laughter and Tisun had to bring them to order.

"But it resolved the case satisfactorily and that's all that counts." He tried to close the subject.

"Satisfactory for whom?" Blue joked.

"Yes, alright, alright. Thanks Fleece. Now a word with you King." Tisun didn't give anyone else a chance until he had seized the chance to bring his friend up to date.

"In fact you will all be interested in this," he started "let's just recap. We know there was the evil entity at the warehouse and what it could do. We also know that it was destroyed, but thanks to the help of our earthly associates we now know that it wasn't before it had started its operation to intercept souls so that they would never find eternal peace. Those souls in turn were saved by another powerful force who is at present readjusting the poor things so that they can progress, but it will take time."

"They were the ones we saw near the warehouse," King cut in but added "some of them were in a sorry state."

"Don't worry," Tisun assured him, "those workers know what they are doing and the trauma will be wiped so that when the souls go on, they won't bear any scars of it in any future existence."

"Guess it's going to take a while with some of them." King was remembering the sights he had seen.

"What's time?" Tisun asked. "As long as the job is done."

They all agreed and looked for the next to speak.

Noodle said he was glad his last stint was over as it had involved food poisoning on a large scale and reiterated his old moan about the way food was prepared and the conditions that customers don't see.

"You talking about the restaurants, or takeaways?" Blue asked.

"Both. I'm telling you, when we are in body we wouldn't go near some of the places, but this is an everyday way of doing things for them."

"So have you brought them to light?"

119

"Very much so, I only have to go sniffing around and someone usually come to see what I'm doing, before I disappear. Only trouble is, that for every one I bring to the attention of the authorities, I bet there's another two or three springing up. We're going to need more of us at this rate."

"Good point," Tisun turned to Cello. "What about you? How's the drink problem?"

The others found that amusing but calmed it down as the Beagle spoke.

"It's the duty free mostly. I've been helping them at the ports. The stuff I've seen trying to be smuggled in, and two noses are better than one. Seen a lot of our old friends as well."

It was Blue's turn and he jumped on this last point

"Yes, the ports and I can tell you about the fags. Was following one chap that seemed to make a few too many coach journeys and he'd brought his legal amount, so did the one with him, and the one behind etc. but they all met up. I followed him because I was curious and they went to a house in the midlands. Well I hovered around there for a couple of days, and they were taking the outer packs, those containing many small ones round in the boot of the car so they were out of sight. So they pull up at an off licence just out of any main city or town, chap goes into the shop and says to the bloke "Got something for you." Then he comes out and buys the duty free from the boot, cash in hand, then he will go and sell them at full price over his counter."

"Now this went on for a while and I noticed he was now going over on the ferry in his car so I suspected there was more than the legal quantity involved, and sure enough there was a very nice little operation going on, and he was increasing the amounts each time. That is until we got him. We let him get away with a few smaller ones then we got him on a big one. Was he mad?"

"Well, you've certainly all earned your stripes," Tisun said then added "Oh, and Mildew is having a great time, he has teamed up with Butch and although they don't give too much away, I think they are both doing the job to which they are best suited."

There was a moment of reflection, then King asked softly, "And what about you boss, what have you got to report, if one may ask?"

After a moment of friendly jeering by the others, Tisun took a deep breath and said "Well I guess I owe it to you to tell you what I know." He was very careful to only divulge the parts that mattered and might affect them, but was aware that Tankard would still like him to be discreet and not want tongues wagging, especially dogs.

It took a moment for the others to realise that Pippa and Ruby hadn't been despatched and they soon were showing signs of elation but Tisun warned them that this was what they mustn't do, so to put it from them and carry on with their jobs unless called in. Although a bit reluctant at first, they were all experienced enough to realise the seriousness of the situation and settled back to their normal mode.

The Ladydogs' task was now quite different. As they grew in strength they had no fear of Raine as they still knew her, and were operating on their own.The paws had implanted the knowledge in them that some evil force was threatening mankind and must be crushed before it brought worldwide devastation and one of its cells was here at the school and must be rooted out.

Redhead's new strength was making her ask questions. She had just left one of her paws sessions and was talking to the other three in the corridor leading to their classroom.

"What gets me, is that if the paws are so powerful themselves, why on earth are we being told to dig it out?"

"I never thought of that." Dinky agreed.

"When I go for my dose at lunchtime, I'm going to ask." Hannah announced.

"Ha, and you think they'll tell you, just like that?" Redhead laughed.

"Well, we've still been programmed to do it I think." Dinky seemed resigned to the fact.

"You're quiet as usual," Redhead turn to the quiet one "how about you chipping in with a few ideas."

"Well I was thinking that we should split up."

There was silence then Hannah asked "Why?"

"Because we could cover more ground. Then when one of us gets a lead, we all join up and follow it."

"Oh, got it all figured out," Redhead almost sneered wishing she had thought of that.

"I...wasn't...um....trying to tell you what to do." The quiet one stuttered.

"Oh that's ok. Good plan. Had you thought beyond it?"

"Well, I wondered if you Hannah would watch Miss Clemence because I'm sure there's much more to her. Um, Dinky, how about keeping an eye on the caretaker, he's tucked away in that boiler house of his and could be up to anything."

Redhead was warming to this and said breezily "And what have you got for me, may I ask?"

"Well, there's quite a few canteen staff and of course it doesn't have to be a single person. It could be a group."

"Good thinking, "Redhead smiled then asked "And just who will you be stalking?"

but thought 'She'll start with 'well' again, I just know it'.

"It may surprise you, but I'm going to be watching the head."

"The head?" was the chorus.

"What on earth for?" Redhead couldn't quite see the reasoning behind this.

"No, not on earth, in spirit. I think she's up to something outside of school but there's a connection here and I'm going to find out what it is."

"And then you will call us in?" Hannah was eager that her sister didn't go it alone once she found a lead.

"Well of course I will. As soon as I find anything."

As the bell rang for start of lessons the three girls made their way into class while Dinky set about looking for the caretaker. She followed the long flight of steps that led down outside to the boiler room and as there was nobody there she had a good look around. There was a small room where he obviously kept his belongings, had his meal and did any paperwork required. Everything seemed in order and she was about to leave when she noticed the bottom draw in his desk was ajar.

"You dirty old beggar!" she laughed as she saw a load of girly magazines stuffed in it, and there were so many the drawer wouldn't close. "I suppose as long as you only look at the pictures, it's Ok." Her mind was drawn back to the reason why she was there.

"If he isn't here, where is he?" she thought for a moment, and after deciding there was nothing here of interest, set off around the school looking for him. As the pupils were all in class it was easy to spot him mending a door on one of the outer buildings. She floated over to have a good look at him, expecting an older man and was surprised to see one possibly only in his thirties but the worry etched on his face made him look much older. As she approached, he stopped and looked straight at her which gave her a bit of a jolt.

"You can see me?" she thought.

"Not exactly." his thought came right back at her.

"But you know I'm here." It was a statement not a question for she knew the answer.

"Very much so. And the others too."

"In what way do you know?"

"I'm surprised you need to ask me that."

She felt he was playing games with her and she wasn't prepared to divulge anything about the Ladydogs but she wanted to know all about him. Maybe this was the lead they had been waiting for.

She moved to the other side of him but his gaze followed her.

"If you can't see me, what sense are you using?"

"You're wasting my time. Don't ask when you already know." He appeared to ignore her and get on with his work.

"Can't we talk?" She moved behind him.

"Why, you got something to say?"

She was getting rather annoyed at his offhanded manner. "I was only trying to be neighbourly, but if you can't be civil, there's no point in talking to you. Goodbye."

He stopped working and turned to face her. "You didn't know I could converse with you, so why did you come?"

"If you're so clever Mr Handyman, you know." Dinky was aware that this was going to be longer than the record rally in any tennis match but felt she mustn't turn her back on it. She had to appear disinterested to keep his attention.

"Stop playing games." He retorted. "If you want to know something, then ask."

She started to float round him in circles. "Don't know if I can trust you."

"Of course you don't."

"How long have you been watching us?"

He almost laughed. "Watching you? You flatter yourself young lady. There's more to watch here than you lot fumbling about not knowing your nose from your tail."

"That's choice. Can't say we've noticed you doing anything useful." She was offended now and wished she hadn't been given this character to investigate. Pity the quiet one hadn't put herself up for it.

He gave her a moment then said very quietly "But that's how you get results. Not charging around being obvious, but just moseying around keeping your head down, and watching."

"Maybe we haven't got time to watch."

"Suit yourself," he shrugged and carried on as if she wasn't there.

Feeling very fed up she made her way back to the classroom. The lesson was about to finish and Clemence was due to take the next so Dinky decided to hang around and be an onlooker. The bell went and the teacher left the room.

"I've come to join you for a bit." She told the others.

Redhead moved over to Hannah as if talking to her. "Why?"

"He knows about us but won't say. Not very helpful." Dinky felt she had to whisper.

"We need to know more about him. He could be the one." Hannah thought.

The quiet one, sitting at the back sent the idea "I think you should stay with him, don't give up, it's the only way you'll find out."

"Probably right, at least until we know for sure." Redhead added. "Don't let him get to you Dink, you're above that."

"If you feel I should." Dinky looked round them all "Ok, if you think so."

The arrival of Clemence halted their communication and Dinky left rather unwillingly to get more information.

Hannah knew she had to trail Clemence after school as she wasn't going to find out much here, unless there was a free period. She tried to look through her timetable but the papers slipped off her desk and she was immediately chastised for not paying attention, so made up her mind to check as soon as possible. If she was free and Clemence was also free, she could lose her body for a short time and spiritually

124

wander around and see if the woman was up to anything. She too wished the quiet one had taken this job and not delegated it.

It was different with Redhead. She was keen to have several people to study and knew she would be busy if she found the need to follow them all after school. It did occur to her that the quiet one must have thought her the best one for this task although she did feel a slight pang at being delegated by the runt. Dinnertime didn't seem the best choice to start as the staff would all be busy with their duties but she may as well give it a go in case they were caught off guard. She would take her paws session later, even after school if necessary and was ready to get her teeth into this as soon as she could.

The quiet one had her plan all mapped out. She was very methodical and sometimes wished the others worked more to a system than the haphazard way they went about things, but that was only her view. They often wanted to throw her organised manner away and tell her to just get on with it, rules or no rules, but she could never change. She had divulged to her sisters that she had written a letter to the head teacher complaining about the way one of the lessons was being taught and had asked for a meeting in confidence with her, and had received a reply that she was to go to the head's office during the afternoon break. The girls had said that they hadn't seen anyone bring a message, but the quiet one said that it had to be done secretly because of the nature of her request and she would let them know how she got on.

"Which teacher did you complain about?" Redhead had wanted to know.

"Who do you think?" was the reply.

Tisun was eager to have another meeting with Tankard as the waiting seemed worse than the years of despair, but he now had more definite things to worry about. It bothered him that his daughters were in the front line and could be targets if the evil felt they were obstructing their progress especially with the increasing power supplied by the paws. It seemed strange that nothing had attacked the paw set up as that surely would have been the obvious objective from the start. He knew all would be revealed eventually, but would there be casualties as a result? But he was only too well aware that he couldn't just summon him and would have to wait until the old dog decided to put in an appearance when he was ready. He considered the fact, that if Mildew could make a quick return from his tandem job, he would send him to the school as that wouldn't seem to be anything unusual. But that also was out of his hands until such time as his pal could be released to come back, even for a visit.

The canteen was very busy and Redhead noticed that there was more going on in the spirit world than on the ground. Each person's body had several attendants, some trying to calm them or offer helpful advice to get through the hectic dinner period but as it progressed and slowed a little, many floated off to other tasks leaving the individual guardians to their own devices. Redhead tried to sift in her mind as to who may be a threat but at this time there seemed to be too much activity to concentrate on anyone in particular, so she decided to come back during one of her classes, when she could appear to be studying but actually drift out and have a look. It was something she often did, and as soon as she felt the tug on her light line she was back in body instantly.

She was about to leave this noisy atmosphere when someone caught her eye. Clearing the dirty plates ready for washing was an assistant quietly going about her business barely communicating with her fellow workers. Physically she would be almost invisible, and as long as she did her job properly, nobody would give her a second thought, but in spirit, it was very different. Hovering round her were several unsavoury characters apparently looking for mischief but using her as a base on which to anchor. Redhead moved round until she was looking into the woman's eyes and was shocked to see the hard image that was looking at her. It was obvious she could see her as she stared back with the unspoken words as clear as if they had been shouted.

"What are you nosing around for? Bugger off!"

Redhead kept her composure and retorted "Why? What have you got to hide I wonder?"

"It's time you amateurs cleared off where you belong and left us alone."

The beings had stopped moving and were all behind the woman and for the first time Redhead saw what a hideous lot they were. Still she held her cool as she looked from one to another trying to work out what kind of image they were portraying, for they seemed to be a mixture of human, animal and something she didn't recognise but it was emitting evil hatred towards her.

"Ok have it your way." She tried to look as disinterested as possible. "I've better things to do than hang around here looking at you lot." and with a passing glance at the woman she moved away slowly.

Once out of the canteen she re-entered her body with a gasp of relief and made her way to the others to relate the experience she just had.

"If you ask me that sounds definitely fishy." Hannah was quick to say.

"I agree, but I still feel that caretaker has a lot more going on than we know." was Dinky's reaction.

"Do you think I really need to watch Clemence?" Hannah had a feeling that she would be on a wild goose chase after hearing these two reports.

The quiet one joined in now. "Of course. We can't dismiss anyone because we think they are not interesting, and don't forget I'm seeing the head in the break."

"Christ, I'd almost forgotten that." Redhead was still full of her own experience.

Quiet one gave her a disapproving look followed by "No need for blasphemy."

"She's getting to be a right little prude," thought Redhead, "are they sure she's one of us?"

They were all eagerly waiting to hear what she had to say after her meeting with the head, but were forced to wait until school finished before they could get into conference.

"Come on, put us out of our misery." was the unanimous call.

Quiet one took a deep breath. "Just as I thought. There's more to her than you could possibly imagine. She has the ideal position, often sitting alone in her office undisturbed. She could be in total control there, and who knows what she is governing."

"Such as?" Redhead wanted to know more.

"I haven't found that out yet, I was only in there a short time. But I shall go again as she wants me to update her on what is going on."

"So you've made her rely on you to spy?" Hannah was trying to work this out.

"You could say that."

"Just a minute" Dinky cut in now "you haven't told us what you said, about Clemence I mean."

Quiet one looked at her seriously "Clemence, did I say it was Clemence? Don't think so."

This took them all aback. She seemed to be keeping them in the dark when they were all supposed to be pooling their knowledge. Redhead wasn't in the mood for being messed about and wondered if this girl should be taking so much charge of things, yet not coming clean about her own details.

"So just who was it you complained about? I think you'd better say so that we all know," she asked her.

"That's not important."

"Well I think it is." Redhead wasn't letting this go now.

Quiet one looked round them all then said very slowly "If you must know, it was about the games mistress."

That seemed to answer all the questions for now and Hannah was the first to say "Of course, she tries to make you do the rough games you hate. Did you tell her it makes you ill?"

"In graphic terms."

This was met with a hoot from Redhead. "You canny little fox, and I bet you were almost in tears."

"She believed me, I even offered to show her the bruises. I pointed out that I bruise very easily and my parents were going to write to her but I had asked if I could see her about it instead."

"That was a bit dangerous, what if she insisted upon a letter from them." Dinky said.

"Oh I'd got that one all ready in case, but didn't need it."

As everyone seemed a bit happier now, quiet one went on to say that there were many souls hanging around the office that didn't have a good aura about them, and after being there for a few minutes, the head teacher's colour changed too. She said that at one point they had surrounded her and she felt very claustrophobic as though they were trying to squeeze the life out of her, while the head just sat there smiling.

"So why does she want you to go back?" Redhead was wondering.

"I'm sure she wants to find out how much I know, so that's why she asked me to report on the games mistress, to get me back there."

"Weren't you scared?" Hannah asked.

"I was, but I'd started this so I knew I had to go through with it, couldn't very well ask one of you to take over. That would have looked fishy."

There was sense to that, but the others were a little amazed at her courage and made her promise that, if things got too hairy, she would get out and they would all take it on board.

It was evening and Hannah had been following Clemence around her small house. The atmosphere was calm and the only spirit presence was the regular guardian who greeted Hannah like a friend.

"Nice to see you. What brings you here?"

"Oh… Oh just seeing if the lady is all right."

The reply came as quite a shock.

"No you're not."

"Then why did you ask?" Hannah felt her back come up.

There was a distinct pause as the two eyed each other up and down before the guardian continued.

"You've been taking quite an interest in her recently haven't you?"

"Oh I know you've been with her at school, but you still let her bully me didn't you?"

"Come on, stop playing games. We all know what that was about, and we also know that she wasn't doing it of her own volition."

"You know quite a lot don't you?" Hannah didn't want to give anything away that she didn't have to.

"You are wasting your time here. You would be better employed looking elsewhere."

"Well, you would say that, if you wanted me to stop nosing about." Then after a moment's thought Hannah asked "You know where to look don't you?"

"All I can tell you is that it isn't here, or anything to do with this lady."

"But you do know something."

The guardian had an air of trust about her which made Hannah feel safe but she beckoned for the girl to leave saying simply "Be careful who you trust dear. Things may not be as they seem."

"But...." Hannah wanted to know more but felt herself being pushed outside the house by this protective spirit, so she had no option but to float back to the school. This seemed a good time to take her paws session, and as there was nobody about she sank into their warm caress for her revitalising moment.

It wasn't long before she realised she wasn't alone but wasn't sure who was with her. As she tried to call out, the words were lost almost as though she had no voice, which was the truth for it was only her spirit that was being recharged, her temporary physical image having been discarded for now.

This was very strange. The sisters had become used to the sensation with each session they had, until it was like a drug and they couldn't wait until the next fix. They visited separately, in pairs or as a group but it was always the same. However there was something different about this and Hannah began to realise that when her sisters were there they were all female, but this presence was very definitely male. As she floated there wondering who it could be, she noticed it was drawing nearer to her until she felt the very strong secure presence entering her very being. She tried to think when, in all her earthly lives, or her entire spiritual being she had experienced such a euphoric feeling of deep satisfaction and renewal and now she was floating on clouds in utter ecstasy. Slowly she was replaced in the paws, and as her awareness returned she felt the male presence leaving her until she was entirely alone recovering slowly from her experience.

Redhead had followed the canteen woman as much as possible, by flitting in and out of body during school time, but when she had the freedom at the end of the day she traced her to a house not far away. At first it seemed to be a normal little place on the outskirts of the town, nothing special but also nothing to attract attention from the outside. But when she floated inside she got the shock of her life.

The place was immaculate and not what you would expect from a canteen assistant. All of the room were well kept in good quality furnishings, very expensive curtains and quite a number of objet d'art housed in secure cabinets. Somehow things didn't add up, so she started looking at the rooms in closer detail.

"Thought you'd turn up sooner or later."

The voice made her jump as she couldn't tell where it was coming from.

"You just had to meddle in what doesn't concern you. And you were warned." The voice was deep and Redhead couldn't tell if it was male or female.

"Who are you?"

"You must know that, or you wouldn't have come here." The voice was mocking now and there was a strong feeling of not being alone.

Redhead now felt herself being pushed along the corridor into a room at the back of the house and although it was dark, her spiritual awareness could make out everything there.

"Oh my God "she thought "devil worshippers."

Everything she was thinking was being picked up by the presence "Nearly right." She heard. It seemed best to keep her thoughts down and force whoever it was to speak next.

"We don't worship the devil. We are the devil."

This put a new light on things, and she wondered if she would get out of this place unscathed but she knew she had been the one to root out the evil that was lurking, waiting at the school.

"So you take your pickings from the girls, and bring them here I suppose." She couldn't resist stating the obvious.

"Very clever." The tone was mocking and Redhead felt she was being played with now and there was much more to this than she first thought. It seemed the sensible thing to try and make her escape but that wasn't going to be easy.

"We didn't think it would take much to draw you here, your nosiness did that." The laughter rang through the entire building. "But as you are here, we may as well introduce you to some of our ways. Pity to waste the opportunity when you so kindly walked straight into our net."

She knew that being on her own she stood little chance against this force, and for all she knew it may be a solitary foe, but a strong one. They kept saying 'we' but that may be a ploy to confuse her.There was a pressure around her back but she wasn't able to determine if it was continual or several different ones, but one thing was certain it was pushing her towards what looked like an altar and she couldn't resist.

The thought was racing through her mind that this may be a control room from which the evil was sending out its waves to spread its force to infect the surrounding area, then push it further afield. Did it have its soldiers placed to react when instructed? That posed the question as to who they were. They could be people going about their everyday lives until activated. But for what?

These questions weren't about to be answered now and she wasn't prepared for what came next. As her soul was lifted and placed on the altar structure, a blinding light came down in a stream from above and snatched her up with such a force, it took her a moment to recover from the action. She didn't know where she was but soon felt the comforting familiar feeling of the paws coaxing her to relax into their power to regain her awareness.

It was around midnight and the dog pack was very busy. Even Tisun had been forced to go out in the field which kept him occupied, but after each job his mind was instantly on the girls and he constantly wondered what progress if any, was being made in tracing the evil presence. He was seriously contemplating sending one of the other lads down in another form so that his daughters wouldn't suspect anything, and try to find out for himself what stage had been reached, but he knew Tankard wouldn't approve and while any intervention could jeopardise the plan, he had no option but to play the waiting game.

He knew that the paws group was protecting them and, although he didn't know the extent of its powers, felt he could trust it to keep them in constant surveillance.

But another strange thing was happening. Although he was getting restless, when he let his thoughts relax he felt he was being updated with messages, and this was something new. At first he chastised himself for filling his mind with worry instead of leaving it open, for with his experience it should have been second nature, but its always a different matter when it concerns those closest to you.

Being on his own, he let himself mentally float, and although his spirit remained at base, he was receiving images of all the girls and knew exactly what had happened to each of them on their quests.

"And about time too."

But this was not his own thought, this came from elsewhere and he knew instinctively that Tankard was nudging him into awareness. So he didn't have to be at the school or anywhere else to know every move being made from now on. Staying in this state, he watched as the four girls met to share the latest information, knowing that Redhead's news would be pointing them in one definite direction.

Helga had only made one brief visit back to the base, and that was when she was sure the girls were out. She paused for a moment, and realised there was no way back for her here for she had lost face and although she felt she had been in power, the reality had hit her that it was all false. She was angry at the so called evil force that had promised to carry out her orders, yet failed, but it brought one thing to light. As they hadn't fulfilled their side of the bargain, they would be in no position to claim payment in any way from her, so in fact she was rid of them. But some of these tiresome beings can make an existence horrendous, even if it's just for their own satisfaction, so she knew she had no option but to remove her entire being from the area and start up again elsewhere. She ploughed through her memory banks.

"Now where was that rather handsome Akita I had my eye on?" The light came back into her being and within seconds she had gone.

The latest development set the girls thinking very seriously about what they were involved in but were reassured that the paws could rescue them at any time. Dinky, Redhead and Hannah were waiting for the quiet one to join them for a combined paws session, but she had said to go in without her if she was late as she was tailing the head mistress to her home. They entered the calming warmth and soon their thoughts were merging and there was a distinct feeling of awareness that they were getting closer than they realised to whatever was threatening. After some time, the quiet one had still not appeared so they emerged to find her just arriving outside.

"I'm glad you didn't wait," she seemed flustered which wasn't like her, as she was always the calm, collected one that kept her cool.

"What happened," Redhead wanted to know straight away.

As the quiet one seemed very reluctant to divulge anything the others started bombarding her with questions, till Redhead silenced them saying she couldn't answer them all at once.

"Alright," the quiet one started, "but be prepared for a shock."

This started another murmuring but they soon let her continue.

"I was going to follow her home, but she didn't arrive."

"What?" was the chorus.

"She drove her car out of town and out to that disused land, the bit that's cordoned off."

"Yes, we know it." Redhead urged.

"Well there was a large van type trailer, and she parked up and walked to it and got inside."

The girls looked from one to another wondering what was coming next.

"What happened then?" Dinky was getting impatient.

The quiet one paused and looked almost guilty then muttered "I don't know."

"What do you mean, you don't know?" Hannah was getting annoyed now. "Didn't you go and look?"

"Of course I did, but that's the funny thing. I got to the trailer and I can't remember any more."

Redhead almost spat out her reply. "Be more specific. Did you go inside the trailer?"

"Not quite."

"Did you or didn't you, it can't be that difficult." Redhead was almost screaming.

"I got to the door and it opened and there were beings inside and I don't remember any more until I found myself back in the area. The trailer and the head's car had gone. I don't know how long I was there."

"That sounds very strange to me," Hannah didn't seem very impressed "you'll be saying you were abducted by aliens next."

"Don't be so silly, I'm not saying anything of the kind."

Redhead took charge. "Well, if what you're saying is true, something took over your awareness and blanked you out, so you were obviously a threat and we can't ignore it."

The quiet one looked a bit relieved. "It wasn't very pleasant, I can tell you, I felt strange, and I couldn't wait to get back here."

"The obvious thing for you to do now is to get into the paws and let them calm you down, then renew your strength." Redhead was in charge and there was something in her order that said she wasn't taking 'No' for an answer.

"You're right, as usual," the quiet one agreed, "just let me settle for a moment, then I'll go in. You all go, I'll be fine."

"Why don't you go now? You know you'll feel better straight away." Hannah couldn't understand the delay.

"She says she needs to settle." Dinky felt sorry for her sister as she looked so vulnerable, then added "as long as you go when you're ready."

"I promise," quiet one nodded then added "thank you."

As the three left, Redhead said "Be back in a min, just got to check on something."

"Now what's she up to?" Dinky laughed.

Hannah looked puzzled. "Don't know, but something's going on."

"Oh not you as well?" but sensing the apprehension in the tone asked "Is it something to do with what that guardian said, what was it now?"

"Things may not be as they seem." Hannah wasn't sure of the exact words but had remembered the gist of it. "Oh and trust nobody, I think. But of course that didn't mean us did it?"

As the two looked at each other, something seemed to click and they both returned to the paws in a second. Redhead was hovering, moving along the extent of the paws but looking confused.

"What is it?" Dinky asked.

"That's funny?" Redhead was still pacing. "She must have gone in straight away, but I thought she wanted to settle first."

All three now focused their attention on the paws.

"Should we wait for her to come out, or go in after her?" Hannah wondered.

There was an uneasy pause as Redhead said quietly "I don't feel there would be any point."

"What?" the others were lost now.

"I'll go if you like, but I don't think she will be there."

"I don't get this." Dinky was getting worried.

Redhead wasn't ready to voice her thoughts but said "Ok, wait here. Promise me you won't go anywhere."

"We won't." both agreed.

"But if she comes out, don't let her wander off until I get out."

The two looked at each other but promised to do as she asked, as she seemed to know what she was doing, whatever it was.

Redhead had only just entered when a disturbance in the air made the others turn.

"What are you doing back here?" the question was light hearted and the quiet one hovered just behind them.

"But we thought you were in there." Dinky was shocked, not only as it was the last thing she expected but the change in quiet one's manner.

"I was. It didn't take long, they're very good aren't they?"

Without thinking Hannah blurted out "But Redhead went in to find you."

"Why would she do that?" again the question was filled with humour.

"Now you tell me." The answer came from Redhead as she emerged and came face to face with the quiet one almost pushing her back. "My, my we have made a quick recovery haven't we?" the sarcasm was cutting the air.

"And you are acting as a detective, following us about, not trusting any of us, when it is you who should be watched. Very clever. Bet she had you fooled." She addressed the others with a smug air about her. Gone was the meek and mild little thing, and they were now looking at someone who was her own person and very much in charge as she hurled the accusation at Redhead.

"What are you talking about?"

Hannah and Dinky were looking from one to the other but Redhead rose above them her face like thunder as she pointed at quiet one.

"I think you've got a lot of explaining to do lady."

136

"I?"

"Yes you, and you know what I'm talking about."

"I haven't got time for this, and nor have you." quiet one spoke to Hannah and Dinky "we have work to do, remember?"

"Just a moment." Redhead's voice growled in such a menacing way, all the others froze. "I think you should explain to us why you don't go into the paws."

"What? But she does, doesn't she?" Dinky was staggered at this.

"Tell them." Redhead ordered.

Quiet one looked from one to the other then sighed. "Oh well, you might as well know. I do go but not when you are around. You see, I've never been as forceful or self assured as you and they gave me special treatment to bring me up to your levels, if you know what I mean."

Hannah gave a visible jump as the words were fed into her soul. "Be careful who you trust dear. Things may not be as they seem."

Simultaneously Dinky saw an image of the caretaker, and he was wagging his finger in a warning gesture. Both looked at each other with the doubt being planted firmly in their souls. Now they turned to the other two and something unseen was guiding them as they said in unison "But we know the truth." and they were gone.

As the two were left alone Redhead was on full steam as she faced the quiet one. "You are feeding them a pack of lies and I know it."

The retort was instant. "You think you are clever, but when they find out the truth, they will see just who the evil one is and who they are working for. It was very clever planting you here after all we weren't told we were related at the start, because none of us would have believed you were one of us."

"You may fool them but you don't fool me. I always wondered why you were such a simpering little thing. I knew you were different."

"That was how it was intended. To draw your attention which it did, because it didn't take long for you to take the bait, and you dismissed the others as not being any threat. But that's where you made your biggest mistake."

"Oh don't try and fob me off with that load of rubbish."

137

"All right. Have it your own way but think on this. While you've been busy watching me, what have the other two been up to?"

For a moment Redhead had no answer, because all that the quiet one was saying was true. She had trusted them all and only taken interest in this girl when she suspected she wasn't entering the paws, which had turned out to be true. But in fact she hadn't followed Dinky or Hannah.

Time for a new approach. "So, miss clever dick, how do you explain my experience?"

"Which one?"

The answer sent a distinct 'ping' in Redhead's mind. If the girl knew everything, she would certainly know about the devil worship incident.

"There was only one." She said very precisely, studying reaction as she split every word as though it was being fired like separate arrows.

"Oh, that one."

Redhead didn't answer or offer any other information but just kept focusing on the so called sister in front of her. She had her on a spot, and knew she had no answer.

"Well, we all know what happened there."

Keeping her composure Redhead replied "Do we?" Then after a moment added "Well, that says it all. Bye." and she disappeared.

Dinky was a bit unnerved by what she had witnessed and felt she must check out the caretaker as soon as she could. The thought that nobody could be trusted was very much to the fore now but she was rather upset if her sisters were involved in something evil, and she felt she must try and get as much information as she could from other sources before jumping to conclusions.

It was Saturday and she wondered if he might be at the school during weekends. It was something she hadn't really thought about until now but it was worth checking out. Hannah had returned to base and Redhead and quiet one were watching each other's every move. Redhead had more questions to fire at her, but first needed to verify a few facts.

Floating towards the boiler room, Dinky slowed her pace as she approached his room.

"Took your time." His deep rumble hit her.

"You'll be telling me you were expecting me next."

"Don't play games, you knew you'd come. You want to know how much I know about the lot of you."

"I never said that."

His shrugged "You didn't have to."

She had stopped near his desk. "Just what do you know, about my sisters?"

"Tunnel visioned."

"They aren't!" she felt a bit offended at this remark.

"Not just them, you."

"Me, I have a very open mind."

"And yet you can't see what's staring you in the face."

This shook Dinky quite a lot and she tried to read what was in his expression, but he could portray utter blankness when he wanted.

"You're all looking for the evil source that's going to destroy everything as you know it."

"Well, what if we are. At least we're doing something about it, not just sitting there."

"You haven't even touched the surface." He turned away and pretended to mend one of his tools.

A sudden thought hit her. "You're here for the same thing aren't you?"

There was no answer so she pursued it.

"You think we're getting in your way don't you? You'd like us to clear off and leave it to you. Well, that's not going to happen."

Now she had his attention but realised she had gone too far. He turned slowly, his eyes penetrating into her.

"Why do you think I'm here?" he snarled.

"I've just said."

"No. You've spoken without thinking it through. Now try again."

"Well, um, you know what we are doing, you have done all along, but I don't know why.......wait a minute!"

He was almost smiling now as he fed the thought into her mind.

She yelled "You are here to protect us!"

"That took you long enough, no wonder you haven't been getting anywhere."

"I must tell the others...."she trailed off.

"Go on, finish the sentence."

"I daren't, I'm not sure of what's going on."

"And you don't know who to believe."

She had to admit he was right. "After what went on between those two, I don't know what to think any more. Hannah's alright though, I trust her."

His head went to one side and the question was on his face before he asked "So why do you think you can trust me?"

This made her stop for a moment. "I don't know, but somehow I do think I can. Oh I'm not sure of anything any more."

There was a long silence then she said "You haven't told me who you are."

"That's not important, and you wouldn't know if I told you. But you have to trust me if you want to get through this."

"What about the others?"

"All will be revealed. But haven't you wondered why you were picked to investigate me?"

This had never occurred to her. She, like the others had taken the reasons for quiet one's choices on common sense, but certainly not on pre ordained planning.

"Can you explain...." but her words were lost in the air, for she was on her own.

Chapter 9

Tisun was picking up a feeling that events were moving and were about to come to a head which caused a mixture of emotions. He felt that Tankard was in some way warning him to be on his guard and stay in charge of his mind regardless of what things may seem. The thought of soon being reunited with his beloved lifted him but his fear for the safety of his daughters made him realise the severity of the matter. He knew that there were always situations such as these as long as there was a threat from evil sources, in fact he had often helped on past operations but something about this was different.

Something was making him relax his being and within a few moments he received a clear message from Mildew.

"Hi there boss, I'll be paying you a visit soon. It'll only be a short one but nice to catch up." and he was gone.

Tisun was on full alert now. This hadn't come through by chance, the pack was being strengthened to full capacity and he wasn't doing it. Next came a communication from Gerald.

"Got the message. Call us whenever."

"This is it," Tisun thought, "they're all being put on stand by, and it can only be on Tankard's orders."

He wished his friend was in a position to contact him personally but he knew only too well, that at times such as these that didn't happen. He scanned the area around the base but all was quiet, then he realised. It seemed too quiet. There was always some sort of activity, either with helpers rushing to scenes of disaster, or souls being helped in transit, but it was too still. Sometimes in special cases, an area would be avoided although no reason would be broadcast, but spirits just took another route without question. Was this what was happening here? But no answers were being given.

As soon as Dinky got back to the paws area, she was joined by Hannah who felt as though her job was done and she was now rather useless. Redhead soon appeared.

"Where is she?" she demanded.

"Not seen her." Hannah said, "and I've been hanging around doing nothing. Can't I tag along with one of you?"

Her question went unanswered as the quiet one seemed to appear from nowhere.

"In case you're wondering, I've just had my session in the paws Redhead." She said in quite a smug tone.

Ignoring her comments Redhead took a position in front of her and paused, staring into her eyes. When she spoke the words were like daggers.

"So, you had a nice chat with the head did you? And then you followed her to the fenced off area did you? And you lost a period of time that you can't account for did you?" Her voice was getting louder with each question but before the quiet one could answer she said "No, No and No."

There was no reaction from the quiet one who remained perfectly composed, but the hatred coming from her was felt by everyone.

Redhead drew closer. "There was no car, no trailer, no beings because you weren't there, in flesh or in spirit." She took a breath before delivering her final blow. "And you haven't been entering the paws. There's always been an excuse and when you have said you were going on your own, you didn't. No wonder you haven't been getting strengthened."

The two others stood there transfixed. Were these the two girls they had known as their sisters? Both were now towering above them growing by the second, Redhead was firing the accusations never flinching for a moment, while the quiet one was silent but her eyes blazed like fire as she tried to fight back with pure silent evil power.

"Get out of her." Redhead's booming voice echoed through the skies around them as she resumed her dog appearance, snarling showing all her teeth and emitting such a ferocious look, it would have taken a very strong force to outwit her.

Dinky and Hannah had drawn back in shock at the unexpected outburst, but what happened next came as an even bigger surprise. The quiet one started to shake, and as an unseen entity left her, she crumpled until she was nothing more than a shapeless mass on the ground. As the two girls edged forward Redhead resumed her human image and ordered "Leave her, just for a moment" then looking up offered a 'thank you' as though she could see who had helped her.

142

"Wh..who was that?" Hannah was trembling.

"Don't know," Dinky whispered but also offered a prayer of thanks as she thought she may know his identity.

After a few moments the quiet one regained her girl form.

"What happened?" she thought rather than said.

"It's alright now. It's gone." Redhead was by her side comforting her.

"I can't think."

"Something took you over, but we've got rid of it. You're you now."

Quiet one looked at the others. "How long was it?"

They both shook their heads. "We didn't know." Hannah whispered.

Dinky turned to Redhead "How did you know?"

Somewhat sheepishly she answered "To tell the truth, I didn't. I thought she was trying to get out of the physical investigating. She's much more of the thinker, planner, you know but not the doer."

Quiet one smiled in agreement. "I'm afraid she's right on that one."

Redhead looked round them all. "I can't tell you what came over me. It was as though something was working through me."

"So are we alright now, I mean has the thing gone?" Hannah still seemed a bit overawed by it all.

"As far as I can tell. But we had better be on our guard."

"Perhaps we should all stick together," quiet one ventured but laughed "Oh am I organising again?"

"Organise away." they all agreed to which Redhead added "It's time for us to act as one, and the first thing I think we need is a communal session with the paws."

"As long as I can be first in," quiet one joked.

It was a very different little set of siblings that took their much needed paws session with their bond restored, but there was much more to it than that, something that only they knew.

Tisun needed a short break to think things through. Aware that things could kick off at any moment he knew he must be able to return to base immediately, but he felt, rather than knew that he had time to converse with his friends Radar and Jack. He timed his visit

143

to coincide when they would both be asleep. Radar knew instantly when he joined them and Jack was alerted from his dream, although not woken.

"Not seen you much, what's been keeping you?" Radar was eying him up and down.

"There's been a hell of a lot. I just needed to clear my mind for a while before, well things may start happening soon."

"Guess you can't tell us." Jack knew the answer but wanted his friend to know he understood.

"That's right. Could really throw a spanner in the works. But it's good to see you guys, say why don't you tell me what you've been doing, I could do with something else to think about."

"Well apart from the warehouse area, most of it's been pretty quiet." Jack started but was interrupted by his dog.

"Come on, he wants to know, stop pissing about and tell him."

This lightened the mood so Tisun looked at the man expecting an account. As he seemed very hesitant Radar continued. "He wants to get married."

"What?" this was the last thing Tisun expected but then asked rather tentatively "Sorry mate, I thought you still were, if you know what I mean."

"I was, but she finally agreed to the divorce so I'm a free man." Jack's face softened.

"Well, come on, who is it?" Tisun pushed, "Anyone I know?"

"Don't think so, but she's a lovely lady, one of the civilian staff."

"And…" Radar was obviously trying to get him to divulge more but Jack didn't seem to be catching on.

"I think you'd better spill the beans feller, doesn't look like he's going to." Tisun was wondering what the big secret was, but he might have guessed.

"Tell him what she's got." Radar was still going for it.

Jack brightened as though a light had been switched on." Oh you mean her dog."

"Her dog! You can't just refer to her as a dog!" Radar was drooling.

Tisun actually saw the funny side now. "Ah, she has a rather attractive little bitch, am I right?"

Jack couldn't resist a dig at his pal. "Do you know, I think he's blushing."

This caused a reaction in Radar. "Don't be stupid, anyway you wouldn't be able to see if I was."

This light hearted moment only lasted a few seconds but it was enough to achieve the period of complete distraction the pack leader needed. Thanking them both he left to await developments.

"What was he thanking us for?" Jack asked

"Can't imagine," was the dog's casual reply, but he secretly wished him all the luck possible as he watched him depart, before the two earth bodies resumed their sleep uninterrupted.

On his return, Tisun was surprised yet pleased to see that Mildew had arrived and all the other dogs seemed to be on the alert.

"What's gone on?" he asked but thought "it would have to be the minute I left that things started to move."

"And hello to you too Mildew," Mildew laughed at the absence of a greeting.

"Oh yes, hello, glad to see you." Tisun was answering but looking around knowing that something was brewing for the air was electric.

No sooner had he settled than Tankard shuffled in, apparently from nowhere.

"Ah, thought you'd be back about now, good timing." He looked round the group. "You lads stay here now. There's always some other group can fill in for you." Nobody queried the fact he seemed to be in control now, but guessed that something was about to explode.

The old dog took Tisun on one side. "You ready for this?" his look was almost scanning him all over.

"It's now? But I didn't think it was that near."

"There's a few things I'd better explain, before they arrive."

"Before who arrives, you've not drawn the evil, whatever it is, to our base?" He was angry at the thought.

"No, wouldn't do that. The evil's been taken care of."

Tisun was almost stuttering, asking two questions at the same time. "How have you taken care of it and what was it?" Then the third question "Who is coming here?"

145

"Calm it lad." Tankard looked round the group. "You'd better all hear this."

Slowly he explained why their leader had been forced to keep much of the knowledge to himself from the Raine/Helga situation and the threat to his daughters, also the fact that Pippa and Ruby were safe. He went on to describe the scenes at the school and the part the girls were playing in trying to detect the evil that was obviously lurking either there or in the area. There were several nervous shuffles amongst the dogs as he progressed and Mildew drew nearer to his friend for support.

"This evil was of the most powerful and destructive kind and only the top dogs, so to speak, would have had the capabilities and know how to get rid of it, maybe not permanently but to scatter it for now."

Tisun was forced to speak. "But you were letting my daughters loose at its mercy!"

"Not quite. You will see." Tankard's voice was now lulling, taking everyone along with the flow of it. We had to get you out of the warehouse situation for your safety, so there would have been no way that we would have put your girls at risk, although they were very important in the whole operation.

Most of the dogs were now totally confused. If the evil had been disposed of, and the two ladies and the girls were safe why weren't they being immediately reunited. There had to be a catch.

The old boy let all this sink in for a moment before he continued. "The evil wasn't actually at the school, but somewhere near."

"What?" was the chorus.

"Oh you're wondering about the various suspects. Shall we clear those up first and get them out of the way?"

"I wish you would." Mildew spoke now "because I never really found anything of any significance there."

"Of course you didn't. Now, who shall we start with, ah yes, Redhead, bright girl that. She hooked onto the canteen woman didn't she, followed her to her house and found what looked like a bit of black magic going on." He paused with the hint of amusement about him.

"It couldn't have been funny for her." King said firmly.

"But she was never in any danger."

"You seem very certain of that."

146

"I am. But let's move on, how about Hannah? She was allocated Clemence, a non starter if ever there was, but one can't take everything at face value."

"You're talking in riddles as far as I'm concerned." Blue was wishing Tankard would come out with whatever he had to say without beating about the bush.

"You still have a lot of patience to learn my friend. This may not be your favourite subject, but listen and learn."

Feeling somewhat told off, the dog had no option but to obey.

"She received a warning to trust nothing." Tankard paused letting the thought sink in that a good force was at work there.

"Moving on," Tankard continued "which would you like me to cover now?" but receiving no answer he said "Dinky I think. She made the acquaintance of the caretaker chappie, who was aware of her presence and they conversed, but she was a bit uneasy as he seemed to know so much about her. But she didn't know whether to trust him or not, and where did he go, I wonder."

"So you must know if she was at risk."

"Ha ha, she couldn't have been in better hands."

Tisun looked at him very closely now. "I want to hear about the other one before I draw any conclusions."

"And so you shall. The quiet one, hmm very apt. Goes about quietly, thinks very deeply but isn't your physical type. Wouldn't want to get in a fight or anything like that. Made up some right tales I can tell you but Redhead sussed her. Also they thought she wasn't getting her fix from the paws but I can tell you she was going there more often than any of the others, and getting more insight into the truth of it. Canny one that."

"Can I ask?" Noodle spoke now "How do you know all this?"

Tisun gave the Beagle a hard look as though he had stepped out of line, but Tankard said "No that's a good question." He motioned for them to gather round before he began.

"It's difficult for you to understand at this level, but if you get higher up you realise why you weren't given the information before." He paused. "Because you wouldn't have had the capacity to comprehend. There are so many things lad that you may never know. Things that you have to take on board without ever getting an explanation. Now, you all have enquiring minds, which is good, but

147

there are many who never ask questions, never have the hunger for knowledge and they have no idea what is going on around them. But I can tell you that what has been taking place around the school would baffle you beyond belief, so let's just leave it at that for now."

There was a moment while all the pack tried to grasp the meaning of his words, and although they still craved the answers, knew he would not explain further.

The dogs looked from one to the other, wondering what was going to happen next, for the air of expectancy was overwhelming.

"Well, this is the moment you thought you'd never see" Tankard turned to Tisun, "she's on her way."

Instinctively the rest of the lads drew back leaving the boss looking out to the skies in the direction of Tankard's gaze.

"There's a bit more I've got to tell you before she comes."

A feeling of hollowness filled the leader's soul. He should have known it wouldn't be that simple, but he was eager to know what his mentor had to impart before Pippa's arrival.

"Go on." he urged.

"You see we've had to play a few trump cards, and it wasn't only your daughters who were our puppets."

"Say that again." Tisun didn't really know what to expect but knew there was no way round it.

Ignoring the request, the old boy carried on. "Well, for a start all the ones they followed weren't evil ones, but clever placings. Yes, that's right, each and every one was put there to guard them so they were never in too much danger. Clemence, the head, the caretaker, and quite a few more."

"For a start?" Mildew questioned.

"Hmm quick aren't you?" Tankard didn't turn but continued "You see Tisun, you didn't only father girls, you had a few lads as well."

There was a stunned silence but they almost guessed what was coming next.

"We used four of your boys as swaps."

Tisun turned to him now. "Just what do you mean, swaps?"

"Oh we swapped them with the girls now and then. Sometimes we were swapping two around that even they weren't sure where they were."

"And during this time the girls were…where?"

Tankard was looking anywhere but at Tisun and he almost shrugged as he said "Oh with their mother."

The gasp that left the dogs almost shook the atmosphere but it was nothing to the emotion coursing through the father of this flock. "So, you are telling me that all this time my girls and boys have been with their mother in a place of safety?"

"And their Aunt Ruby, don't forget her." The reply was curt."

This time Mildew sidled back up to Tisun and leant on him slightly to give him support, as he knew this would be knocking the stuffing out of him and he needed to be strong for the emotional reunion that was about to take place in front of them.

"I take it that's all." he asked almost weakly.

All faces were on Tankard now. "I don't suppose it will hurt to tell you now it's all over."

"Tell me what?"

"Oh there was evil alright, but not at the school. That was never the source and it was never in danger," then apologetically "as were any of your children."

For once Tisun was lost for words with all reasoning and emotion draining from him. The others were muttering amongst themselves but Mildew spoke for his friend.

"Then what was all the anguish, the sickening worry for. Why did he have to go through this?"

"Because if he had known he wouldn't have reacted the same way and he was being watched, as were you, the girls, and the paws."

"Oh yes the paws. How do you explain those?"

"Simple tricks we know."

Tisun cut in here. "I notice you didn't mention the boys. Weren't they being watched as well.?"

"Boys? There were only girls at the school."

"Now wait a minute, you said they swapped."

"Ah, you see, you believe what you think you know. Because I told you they had swapped, in your mind you saw boys, but don't forget they would still have the images of their sisters. So the evil would not be watching boys, now would they?"

"Ok, Ok" King stepped forward "Please explain why they were watching the school at all."

"Because we wanted them to."

"Oh this get's more confusing as it goes on." Blue whispered.

"I told you we hadn't finished with them, because they were a perfect distraction. While the evil was certain that something was going on at the school, we were able to...shall we say execute our plan to dispose of them in one complete operation. I hate those that straggle on and we have to keep going back to pick up the odds and ends."

"There was never a threat." Tisun was still trying to put the pieces in place. "All that and there was no danger."

"Oh don't underestimate it, everything could have gone horribly wrong, but they played their parts to perfection."

"But they didn't know that. They thought they were fighting evil."

The next reply hit the leader like a brick. "Well then, be grateful it all turned out alright."

Before Tisun could utter the tirade that came to mind, Tankard indicated ahead of them. "Here she comes."

Again the other dogs fell back behind them, leaving a clear view of the approaching image, but all tails were wagging in excitement.

Like a huge ivory bird they came, with the beautiful white German Shepherd Pippa at the head. On her right side as if they were forming the top of the wing was Dinky accompanied by her brother Delta and balancing on the left was Hannah with Kappa. Near the end of the right wing was Redhead alongside Rho, and on the left Quiescence, to give quiet one her proper name, with Upsilon. Ruby was flying in the tail position. All were in the mother's livery and as the sun caught the image, tears rolled unashamedly down Tisun's face, for he had never seen such a beautiful sight in his entire being. Tankard moved back to join the pack as Ruby and the children did the same leaving the two lovers together as they all knew this was a very private and emotional moment.

Before their gaze the two entwined their colours of white and black spiralling together as they rose way into the heavens to spend indescribable moments together, moments they both believed they would never share again.

This would make a beautiful ending, and if you wish you may now close the book and the story is over. But many readers say that books finish too abruptly and they wanted to read more, so for those of you who haven't had enough, the next little chapter is just for you.

Chapter 10

Having no idea how long the two would spend on their 'honeymoon', Tankard beckoned Ruby and the children over to the base. It didn't take long for them all to be in conversation about their work and the sons were eager to learn of the dog pack's exploits hoping they may be able to join them and leave the girls to do girls things.

Tankard cut in to remind them that the pack was of high calibre and you didn't just walk in and be one of them. It took a lot of training, experience but mostly natural instincts.

King felt he had to question this old dog about his speech. "You drop that accent to suit yourself, but you never change your image."

"Don't I? Well fancy that."

"That's right isn't it? I haven't seen you change since you came."

At this point Dinky overheard and added "Pardon me but I think you have."

"Oh and when would that be?"

"You know very well you old buzzard," she laughed. "you were the caretaker, weren't you?"

He scratched his head. "No, I don't think I've ever been a caretaker."

"Yes you were, I'm sure of it."

He eyed her as though he could see right through her. "And just where might that be?"

"At the school of course."

"School? What school?"

She was getting impatient with him. "The one we were all at silly."

The others started taking notice now and the girls joined in.

"The one where the paws were." Redhead laughed.

"No. Can't say I know of one with any paws."

Quiescence sidled up and whispered "You know very well where the school is."

Tankard said loud enough for them all to hear "Supposing you all think about it and I'll pick up on your thoughts."

"Ok" the girls and boys agreed and concentrated their thoughts to the school.

Tankard laughed as he made his way to leave.

"Well now I'll show you just where you've been, where you've really been that is."

In front of them was the view of a piece of waste ground. Where the school buildings had been lay piles of old concrete, while the head's office was nothing more than a pile of rotten wood.

"I don't understand," Hannah was lost."

"Think I do" Ruby joined in. "He is one clever master of illusion. He could make you believe anything he wanted which is why he is so good at what he does."

They turned to speak, but he had gone.

"I'm not sure if he was here at all." Redhead whispered.

"Nobody ever is," Ruby was looking wistful, hoping that one day their paths would cross again.

"I wonder what they are talking about" Hannah whispered looking up to the point where their parents had mingled with the clouds.

The dog pack looked amused and Cello whispered for only them to hear "Never mind the talking. Guess there's be a few more brothers and sister coming along soon."

"Well, as long as they are happy." The girls sighed.

"Oh, they be 'appy alright" Fleece did the best impression he could of Tankard which sent the pack into a round of 'boys' laughter.

Tisun and Pippa were now finally as one, but sorry, the rest is private!

It is only fair to give the spirit dogs the last word, whether they are in earthly form for their awareness is ongoing, or purely in spirit.

"The dogs never divulge their special secrets for obvious reasons and as long as there is a call for help, their work will never be done.
Thank you for enjoying the experience of our special world."

About the Author

Tabbie Browne grew up in the Cotswolds in central England which is where she gets the inspiration for her novels. Her father had very strong spiritual beliefs and she feels he guides her but always with a warning to stay in control of your own mind.

Her earliest recollection of writing was at primary school and it has seemed to play a part at significant times during her life. She thinks it is only when we are forced to take step back and unclutter our minds for a while we realise our potential. This point was proved when she slipped a disc, and being very immobile had to write in pencil as the ink would not flow upwards! At this time she wrote many comical poems which, when able again, performed to many audiences. Comedy is very difficult but you know if you are a success with a live audience.

In 1991 as a collector of novelty salt and pepper shakers, she realised there was no book in the UK devoted entirely to the subject. So she wrote one. Which meant she achieved the fact that it was the first of its kind in the country and it sold well to like collectors not only in the UK but in the USA.

Another large upheaval came when she was diagnosed with breast cancer, and due to the extreme energy draining, found it difficult to work for an employer. So she took a freelance journalist course and was pleased to have articles accepted, her main joy being the piece about her father and his life in the village. Again the inspiration area.

But the novels were eating away inside and drawing on her experience at stamp and coin fairs she wrote *A Fair Collection* which she serialised in the magazine 'Squirrels' for people who hoard things.

When she wrote *'White Noise Is Heavenly Blue'* and its sequel *'The Spiral'* she sat at the keyboard and the titles just came to her, as did the content of the books. There is no way she could write the plot first as she never knew what was coming next, almost as if somebody was dictating, and for that reason she could never change anything.

Loves:
Animals,
Also performing in live theatre and working as a tv supporting artiste.

Hates:
Bad manners,
Insincere people.